HAMISH
AND THE WORLDSTOPPERS

For EB and Clo.
With all my love.
Danny Wallace

For my sister Nicole,
and her face.
Jamie Littler

First published in Great Britain in 2015 by Simon and Schuster UK Ltd
A CBS COMPANY
Text copyright © Danny Wallace 2015
Illustrations copyright © Jamie Littler 2015
Design by Paul Coomey

Simon & Schuster UK Ltd · 1st Floor, 222 Gray's Inn Road, London WC1X 8HB
www.simonandschuster.co.uk

A CIP catalogue record for this book is available from the British Library
PB ISBN: 978-1-4711-2388-7
HB ISBN: 978-1-4711-2387-0
eBook ISBN: 978-1-4711-2389-4
Printed and bound by CPI Group (UK) Ltd, Croydon, CR0 4YY
Simon & Schuster Australia, Sydney · Simon & Schuster India, New Delhi
4 6 8 10 9 7 5 3

HAMISH

AND THE WORLDSTOPPERS

DANNY WALLACE
ILLUSTRATED BY JAMIE LITTLER

SIMON & SCHUSTER
LONDON   NEW YORK   SYDNEY   TORONTO   NEW DELHI   STARKLEY

St

January 21st Wednesday 2015 vol 7 issue

TOWN CLOCK STILL FAST

WAS THAT A MOtH?

Did anyone see a moth in the window of Slackjaw's Motors last Tuesday?

"It was either a moth or a small piece of beige plastic," says Starkley resident Lorna Boom. "I didn't really get a very good look at it as I had a hair appointment at British Hairways with Diane who usually cuts it but she was on holiday so Barry did it in the end."

Diane returned from holiday just this morning but was unavailable for comment on whether it might have been a moth or a small piece of beige plastic, because she had to stay in and wait for a small piece of beige plastic to be delivered. (She recently lost one while test-driving a second-hand Volvo).

news&cooking

The big clock in Starkley Town Square is still running fast, an expert with a watch has revealed.

"I stood there, completely still, for what seemed to be a very long time – and the minute hand just shot forward!" he said. "Something must be done!"

There are no plans to do anything.

SOMEONE LOSE A PENCIL?

A pencil was found near a bin on Monday.

"We're hopeful we can get it back to its owner, whoever that may be!" said PC Saxon Wix. "We will stop at nothing to make sure it is returned!"

The pencil is described as yellow with

an eraser on one end, and is pencil-shaped. "It is standard pencil-length," says PC Wix, "and has the name MANJIT SINGHDALIWAL down one side."

The police are appealing to the public for any information that might help.

POTATO LOOKS A BIT LIKE DOG

Starkley resident Tinky Patel thought readers mig be interested in a picture took of a small potato he says looks like a dog.

"It looks like a dog," says Mr Patel. "Even though it's just a potato. Wait there, I'll get it."

Mr Patel couldn't find the photo in the end, but says the potato really does look like a dog.

ELEVEN O'CLOCK LULL IN MINI-MART

There were no shoppers in the mini-mart at eleven o'clock on Monday, although a shopper did come in at just a few minutes past, reports say.

"He bought a Choc Ice and two eggs," said a shocked Mrs Fimble. "It was all very eerie. I just stared at him."

Everything was back to normal by Tuesday.

wOMAN DIALS WRONG NUMBER

It was an unusual evening for Starkley dentist Eric Fussbundler last Monday as he answered his telephone to hear a woman asking for "Maureen".

"But there isn't a Maureen in the house," explains Eric. "So I had to tell her she must have dialled the wrong number! She was ever so apologetic and I didn't hear from her again, so I can only assume she finally got through to the Maureen in question. You just don't expect that kind of thing to happen round here. They must have had ever such a laugh about it!"

PRICE 65p

MAN VISITS WRONG SHOP

Old Mr Neate from lumroot Alley meant walk into the bakers day – but walked into e butchers instead!

"As soon as I real-d my mistake I walked into the kers," said Old Mr ate, laughing.

The story certain-made the rounds. It n became the most ular story of all time e Starkley Post website – even beat-ing UNUSUAL YEL-LOW CAR IN TOWN and WHAT'S THAT SMELL?

STARKLEY COUNCIL CONSIDER-ING NEW PRINTER

Five years ago Star-kley Council bought a new office printer from Alan Cartridge in Frin-kley and plans are afoot to replace it.

"It's very early stages but I can confirm that we are considering the possibility of may-be investing in a new colour printer," said spokesperson Tiffany Ramp. "But of course we may not as the cur-rent printer is absolutely fine."

Last year the Council invested in a new mouse mat – a luxury that local teacher Ever Longblather called "madness".

1

What on Earth?

Hamish Ellerby's eyes were the size of satsumas as he sat completely still in his chair.

And he sat completely still because he was totally, utterly petrified.

This was so strange.

What on earth was going on?

Seriously – what on *earth*?

It had all happened in an instant. The scariest, coolest, most awful, most brilliant, most horrible, most wonderful thing.

Hamish wanted to get up and look around. But he couldn't. He was too frightened even to move a single muscle.

This was *incredi*-weird!

Just a matter of moments ago, gangly Mr Longblather had been leaning forward onto a desk using just his knuckles, the way he always did when he was about to ask Class 4E of Winterbourne School a question.

'Who can tell me about soil erosion?' he'd said, and everybody's hearts had sunk at once, because if there's anything more boring than soil erosion then no one's told me about it. Mr Longblather was one of those particularly boring teachers, with a particular talent for making particularly boring things even more particularly boring than normal. In this respect, at least, Mr Longblather was absolutely extraordinary.

When the question had been asked, Hamish had stared down at his pencil case and made his special *ooh-let-me-think* face. He ran his hand through the thick black hair his mum called 'The Mess' and squeezed his huge greeny-brown eyes shut, like he was really trying to come up with an answer. Sometimes he found this was enough to convince people he was thinking about soil erosion. (Fact: Hamish had never really thought about soil erosion. It was not something he was all that concerned about. To be honest, he didn't even really know what soil erosion was.)

'Soil erosion!' Mr Longblather had repeated, now looking a little peeved. 'Come on, **4E!** Soil erosion!'

Mr Longblather had then put his hands on his hips and sighed a deep sigh. Hamish kept looking at his pencil case. 'Surely **SOMEONE** knows **SOMETHING** about—'

And there he had paused . . .

And Mr Longblather's pause continued.

This was quite a dramatic pause, Hamish had thought. It would be a good pause to have in a soap opera or a TV talent show, he decided. But the pause would be over soon, because pauses always end, don't they? That's why they're a pause and not a stop.

But this pause went on.

And on.

And on.

And then on some more.

In fact, no one said anything for ages. The class had never been so quiet. It was *reeeeally* very awkward.

So finally, Hamish raised his head and put his hand up.

But nothing happened.

Mr Longblather didn't say, 'Hamish Ellerby, you wonderful pupil, please tell us everything you know about soil erosion.'

And he didn't say, 'Hamish Ellerby, you are the saviour of this school, the greatest child in all the land, and possibly a future world-famous expert in the field of soil erosion.'

He didn't even say, 'Come on then, Hamish, spill the beans!'

Mr Longblather didn't say anything at all.

And that was when Hamish realised something was just a little bit wrong. Because when he finally looked up, Hamish could see that Mr Longblather was completely and utterly still.

Frozen.

A statue.

Immobile.

Not moving.

Stuck.

Stuck stuck.

Well, this is odd, thought Hamish. He frowned and studied his teacher a little closer. Mr Longblather's mouth was wide open, his fat pink tongue hovering near his two front teeth. Mr Longblather had a very thin, very droopy moustache that sort of looked quite sad to be there. It was so long it looked like it was trying to escape from his face. Hamish could see some drool glistening between its thin, brown, wiry hairs.

And then Hamish noticed something even odder, if that was at all possible.

A tiny ball of spit was hanging in the air just a few centimetres from Mr Longblather's mouth. It caught the sunlight and glistened like a miniature star.

It wasn't unusual for Mr Longblather to shower his class with spit, of course. He was one of those teachers who spits when he talks. You know the type. The teacher that makes everyone fight over the seats at the back of their class. In fact, Mr Longblather was such a repeat offender of unwanted spittle-distribution that Astrid Carruthers's mum even let her bring an umbrella to class. But it *was* unusual for a blob of the icky liquid to be stuck in mid-air.

How was it just hanging there? It was fascinating! It made Hamish want to reach out and touch that little wet ball. This was probably the first time in his life he had ever actually wanted to touch someone else's spit.

He turned to see if the rest of 4E had noticed this little spit-star too, which is when he saw what *really* shocked him.

They were all perfectly still too!

Nobody was moving.

The school bully, Grenville Bile, had one grubby, tubby little finger halfway up his nose and was making a face like he'd just smelled some really awful cheese.

But he wasn't moving.

Colin Robinson had one skinny leg raised slightly off the ground and a very guilty look on his face.

But he wasn't moving.

Brainy old Astrid Carruthers had her hands tightly gripped around the umbrella under her desk, ready to press 'Open' – just in case Mr Longblather turned to ask her a question and showered her in a monsoon of spittle.

But Astrid Carruthers did not move one centimetre.

Hamish started to sweat.

'Hello?' he said, but no one said hello back. His voice sounded enormous in this deathly silent classroom. 'Hello…?'

Next to him, his friend Robin was mid-blink. He looked like a photograph you'd probably want to delete.

Hamish was starting to panic now. He looked out of the window and saw the school caretaker, Rex Ox. Maybe he could call out to him . . . But then Hamish realised Rex Ox's feet seemed to be planted to the ground and his broad shoulders were perfectly still. The bright orange leaf blower he had in his hands was silent.

And my goodness, look! Leaves were *stuck in the air* all around him!

And there – over there, by the bins – a cat was leaping between two walls, except it was just sort of floating in mid-air!

It looked like some kind of weird cat balloon.

And then Hamish pressed his hands up against the window and stared up into the sky . . . because there was a plane! Stopped still! Like it was pinned to two clouds that weren't moving either!

Hamish's eyes struggled to take everything in. They were getting wider and wider and wider and wider . . .

What should he do? What do you do when *the whole world stops*?

His mind raced. *Come on, Hamish, think!* He was a bright

kid. He read a whole book about gravity once. He could spell 'malovalent'.

I mean 'melovelant'.

I mean 'milevolunt.'

Never mind! What I mean is, Hamish could spell *loads* of words.

So was this a test? Or a dream? Or a joke? April Fool's Day was *last* month.

But was everyone in on this? Was Hamish Ellerby being made a fool of?

Surely this weirdness was too much for a ten-year-old to deal with? So Hamish made a very important decision indeed. He knew just what to do.

He would just do what everybody else was doing.

Which was absolutely nothing at all.

So Hamish just sat there. Quietly. Confused. Every now and again glancing at the clock on the wall, which was actually completely pointless, because the clock had stopped too.

And the longer the pause became, the more Hamish began to realise that he was very, very afraid.

What if the world never starts again? he thought, alone in the silence. *What if this lesson about soil erosion just goes on and on forever?*

He noticed his hands had begun to gently tremble. He felt a bit like crying now. If the world never started again, he would be the only boy who could move in the whole of Starkley. Who would he play with? Would he ever be able to speak to his mum again? What if she'd stopped still too? Who'd make him sausage and mash? Who'd give him money for Chomps? But wait – worse than that . . . what if this was the *end of the world*?

Hamish's tummy turned and swirled like it had a badger in it. A very turny, swirly badger. One with a severe nervous condition and no real control of its legs.

And still he waited.

And then, after what could have been a minute or an hour or a *whole month* later . . .

'*—SOIL EROSION!*' Mr Longblather shouted, which startled Hamish so deeply his knees slapped against the roof of his desk. Then he felt that little shooting star of spit finish its journey and slop right on the end of his nose.

But Hamish didn't care! There was *movement*!

The clock ticked again like nothing at all had happened. Somewhere a bell rang. One of Mr Longblather's hairy knuckles cracked on the desk.

Hamish glanced at Grenville, who was still foraging in his

nostrils, trying to find what he always called the 'fruits of my nose'. Outside, cars motored by. The cat landed safely and dashed behind some bins which rattled and rocked as she knocked them. Fat brown leaves danced around Rex Ox's head as the leaf blower roared.

Hamish felt such relief. Trees were swaying, shadows shifting, planes flying, clouds floating, wind blowing . . . and Mr Longblather still waited for his answer.

'I am *perfectly* happy to keep asking until the end of time!' he said, grumpily.

And then everybody laughed as Colin Robinson farted.

2

Boring!

The best thing to do, Hamish decided, was just not to think about it.

Why dwell on it? Dwelling on it was too worrying. Especially because . . . well . . . weird things like pauses that lasted forever didn't happen in Starkley.

In fact, exciting things *never* really happened in Starkley.

An interesting fact about Starkley is that there are no interesting facts about Starkley.

It was a small town right on the coast, meaning most of the cars that came into Starkley simply did a U-turn and drove off again. You could sit on the bench by the big clock and just watch cars arrive in town and then turn round again. Lots of people sat and did that on Saturdays, because there wasn't that much else to do.

To be honest the most exciting thing that had ever happened in Starkley was when it was voted Britain's Fourth Most Boring Town. This was a *great* day in Starkley.

'Fourth Most Boring!' people had said. 'We've arrived!'

Someone had suggested having a party in the church hall to celebrate. But it was cancelled, because someone else didn't fill out the correct health and safety forms.

Booooring!

But what's more is that everyone agreed being voted *fourth* most boring town actually made Starkley *even more boring* than the town that won *first* prize. Because at least that town had won an award and winning an award is pretty exciting. That made the town that won a *billion* times less boring than Starkley! Everyone seemed quite proud that Starkley wasn't even boring enough to be named the most boring town in Britain – and that made it *incredibly* boring.

In fact, do you know what? If you think *your* hometown is boring, here are the three top news stories on the *Starkley Post*'s website:

LOCAL MAN ACCIDENTALLY WALKS INTO SOMEONE ELSE'S PHOTOGRAPH

This was the story of a man who had accidentally walked into someone else's photograph. He had dipped his head slightly when he did so, which he seemed to think meant he wouldn't show up in the picture. But he did.

Boring!

MRS PIPPERKIN SLIGHTLY BURNS CAKE (BUT IT'S FINE AND ALMOST NO ONE NOTICED)

This one had kept the town talking for a while, because Mrs Pipperkin did not normally burn her cakes, so everyone was quite relieved that it had turned out okay.

Bo-*ring*!

BOY SEES FLY, OPENS WINDOW

Hamish didn't bother reading that one. He felt like he could probably guess what it was about.

Super-ultra boring!

So Hamish just decided to try and ignore the fact that the world had stopped earlier that day. It would blow too many people's minds. No one would know how to cope. And anyway, ignoring it had worked perfectly well the first time it had happened.

Yes, that's right. I said 'the first time it had happened' . . . Because Hamish had a secret. Something he didn't even really want to admit to himself.

Hamish had noticed the world stop once before.

He hadn't told his mum. And he didn't want to tell his

older brother Jimmy, who was fifteen and was far too busy trying to grow a wispy moustache and take pictures of himself looking cool and moody on his phone to listen to anything Hamish had to say. So the first time Hamish thought he'd seen the world stop, he'd kept it to himself. He was worried it might make him sound odd. Some of the kids at school already thought he was odd, without him telling them about strange world-stopping things.

The first pause he'd noticed had been two weeks ago. He had been in his garden at thirteen Lovelock Close. It was evening, the sky was dark purple and the only light was from the windows inside.

Hamish had seen a strange shape hanging in the air. It was maybe six feet off the ground.

Hamish knew what six feet was, because his dad was six feet tall. His dad was always saying 'I'm the tallest man in the world!' and stretching himself even further. Hamish loved that, but he knew his dad wasn't the tallest man in the world. That was Mr Ramsface next door. He looked like a big string bean.

Hamish had stared at the mysterious shape in the garden, then moved slowly towards it. He wondered what on earth could be so quiet and still like that.

14

He moved closer, treading gently on the grass in case he disturbed whatever it was.

And when he got really close, he was amazed.

It was a blackbird.

Its mouth was open. Its wings were spread. But it did not move.

Hamish had quietly studied its dark yellow beak and the grooves on its feet. He could see his own reflection in its shining eyes.

It was beautiful.

And for a second it seemed as if Hamish and the blackbird were simply staring at one another.

And then . . .

FAF-FAF-FAF-FAF-FAF-FAF-FAF . . .

The bird flapped away and rose high into the sky, gliding up over the trees and across the moon.

Hamish had watched it go, then walked inside. His mum had been asleep on the sofa after another long day at work. A fine line of drool trailed from her mouth to a cushion like a slimy rope bridge and she was making that exhausted snorey noise mums make, but pretend they don't. Jimmy was on the sofa next to her, but barely looked up. He was too busy pretending to know all the answers on *Britain's Brainiest Boffins and Brainboxes*.

So no. Hamish had not told anybody about the magic blackbird. The only person he would have told was his dad. He knew his dad would have been amazed. His dad would have been delighted.

He really missed his dad.

'HEY YOU!' shouted someone, very loudly indeed.

Hamish stopped thinking about the blackbird incident and looked around. He was maybe halfway home from school, just past Slackjaw's Motors.

'YOU! HAMISH!'

Hamish saw who it was.

Oh, no. Keep walking!

'C'MERE!' shouted another voice. **'I WANT TO TALK**

TO YOU, YOU LITTLE **PIGSWIGGLER!**'

It was stinky little Scratch Tuft. And lolloping behind stinky little Scratch Tuft was the awful Mole Stunk.

They were the *worst*. They were slippy, snidey, slimy little snakes with cruel eyes and pinched faces. And worse still, if Scratch and Mole were here, that meant Grenville Bile wouldn't be far behind.

Grenville Bile, who thought all his flab was pure muscle.

Grenville Bile, who was always after the 'fruits of his nose'.

Grenville Bile, who thought he was so good at wrestling he could probably go to America and earn billions and billions, but said he wanted to stay at school so he could get his geography GCSE first.

Grenville Bile . . . the Postmaster's son!

'YOU LITTLE WORMPIDDLER!' yelled Mole.
'STAY WHERE YOU ARE!'

Hamish stopped walking and straightened his back to make himself look braver. He hated Scratch and Mole. Why wouldn't they just leave him alone? Scratch and Mole were the type of kids who trap spiders in jars and shake them while their skinny little legs clack together in glee. They were the type of kids who pee in bottles and leave them at bus stops in case anyone's thirsty.

They were the worst girls *ever*.

And Hamish knew what they wanted. They wanted his Chomp bar.

Hamish always carried a Chomp bar with him and Scratch and Mole were always trying to steal it. Sometimes they'd take it straight to Grenville as an offering. Scratch worshipped Grenville so much she had a poster of him on her wall. Mole worshipped him so much she'd found her birth certificate, scribbled out 'Mole' and written 'Grenvilla' on it instead, but apparently that didn't count.

Sighing, Hamish felt in his pockets, ready to give up his chocolate bar. But disaster! It was nowhere to be found! Then he remembered – he'd eaten it at lunchtime. His Chomp had been chomped!

Seconds later, they were right in front of him. Even stretching out on their spindly little legs, they only came up to his nipples. Hamish caught a whiff of them. The rumour was that they smelled so bad that even stink-flies flew away from them, coughing and trying not to inhale.

'I'm afraid I ate my Chomp already,' explained Hamish, who couldn't stop himself being helpful even at times like this.

'SHUDDUP!' yelled Mole.

'SHUT YER MOUTH HOLE!'

Their tiny hands were rifling through his bag now.

Then his pockets.

Then his other pockets.

Hamish started to wish the world would stop again. He could escape, like the blackbird, if that happened. The girls would think he had simply vanished.

Wait . . . what if . . . ?

Hamish shut his eyes. If *he* could stop the world, that would be the coolest thing ever!

So as Mole Stunk and Scratch Tuft pulled at his sleeves, checked in his socks and turned him right the way around . . . Hamish *wished*.

He wished hard.

He wished that the world would stop.

He wished that the world would stop right now!

He wished and wished and wished and suddenly all was very, very quiet indeed . . .

He kept his eyes squeezed shut. Had he done it? Was he in control? Could it be true?

Then he heard someone clear their throat.

'Ach—eeeeeeeeeeem.'

He opened one eye. Mole and Scratch were just staring at him.

'WHY YOU GOT NO CHOMPS?' spat Scratch. 'YOU BETTA GETTA **LOTTA** CHOMPS TOMORROW!'

'YEAH!' yelled Mole. 'YOU BETTA GET LIKE TWO **MILLION** CHOMPS BY TOMORROW BREAKTIME! OR ELSE WE'LL SQUIDDLE YOU LIKE A DIDDLER!'

'THASS RIGHT!' screeched Scratch. 'WE'LL MUFFLE

YOU UP LIKE A PING–PONG BALL!'

Hamish just stood there and blinked while the stinky little girls grunted their way around him. Two *million* Chomps? That was loads! That was more than he could eat in a *week*!

And two seconds later those dreadful, horrific little things ruffled his hair until it was all messed up and ran off cackling.

Hamish knew they were probably going to tell Grenville Bile all about it.

Tomorrow at school would *not* be fun, he decided.

Little did he know it then, but tomorrow at school would be something else entirely.

3

The Explorer

At 13 Lovelock Close, Hamish's mum was sitting down with the *Starkley Post* and eating her favourite biscuits.

The story on the front page was

MAN LEAVES TOWN, WILL PROBABLY COME BACK IN A BIT

'Would you like a chocolate Mustn'tgrumble, Hamish?' she asked.

No way, thought Hamish. *Mustn'tgrumbles are disgusting. They taste like sawdust and soil.* Hamish couldn't work out why more people didn't grumble about Mustn'tgrumbles.

'Do we have anything else?' he asked, innocently, walking to the cupboard. Maybe Mum had gone mad and bought two million Chomps. You never know.

But the cupboard was bare.

'I need to run to Shop Til You Pop,' said his mum, looking annoyed at herself. She'd just been so busy lately. Hamish's mum worked at Starkley Town Council, in the Complaints Department – and that used to be the easiest job in the world, because no one ever had much to complain about in Starkley.

But lately, for some strange reason, things had been getting a lot busier. Only slowly at first. But, more and more, people were finding things to be grumpy about.

Mr Slackjaw of Slackjaw's Motors kept complaining, because he was sure that someone kept borrowing his mopeds at night.

And Madame Cous Cous, who ran the sweet shop, kept complaining that people sometimes asked for one sweet and then changed their mind and asked for another and **THAT MEANS THEY SHOULD BE FORMALLY CAUTIONED AND THEN THROWN INTO JAIL.**

Hamish's mum thought that might be taking things a bit far. But she had to take every complaint seriously. Although there was so much paperwork to do that sometimes she felt like lodging a complaint herself.

(She never did, because she knew that would just mean *even more* paperwork.)

Hamish's mum ruffled his hair.

'I'll get you a couple of Chomps if that's what you're after. Or you could use your pocket money?'

Hamish got £4 a week for doing odd jobs around the house. This is what he usually spent it on.

40p: two Chomps from **MADAME COUS COUS'S INTERNATIONAL WORLD OF TREATS.**

£1.50: the latest issue of the Captain Beetlebottom comic. Captain Beetlebottom was awesome. He had a beetle's bottom! Though he also had the nose of a pony – so Hamish often wondered why he wasn't called Captain Ponynose instead.

£1: a ride on the Gap-toothed Otter. That was the greatest rollercoaster since the legendary Vomit Comet! Because Starkley was right by the sea, it was always the last place the travelling funfair stopped. It always parked up in a field by the woods, next to Farmer Jarmer's sunflower field. And the Gap-toothed Otter was the biggest, tallest, spindliest, scariest ride of them all. Hamish would save all year round so he could go on the Gap-toothed Otter as many times as possible whenever the fair came to town. His record last year was twelve rides! It would have been thirteen, but he was sick in a bin and had to go home.

£1: a charitable donation to the elderly gentleman who looked after the town clock and who had fought in the war.

And 10p he saved for his old age. Hamish was pretty sensible like that.

This week, though, he knew he was going to have to spend the whole lot and even maybe dip into his old-age fund too. All to make sure Scratch and Mole didn't squiddle him like a diddler.

Hamish glanced out of the window.

His next-door neighbour, Mr Ramsface, was playing cricket on his driveway with the two miniature Ramsfaces. The Ramsfaces were a strange little family who all played the ukulele together at night and sang unusual songs about boats. Sometimes it was the last thing Hamish heard at night. He would pretend he found it annoying, but actually he thought it was quite lovely.

Little Billy Ramsface really only talked about giant squid, which made conversation quite tricky. Little Betty Ramsface really only talked about hens and why they all should wear little hats. Mrs Ramsface wrote very long folk songs about nothing in particular, while Mr Ramsface made weird costumes out of household rubbish, just to make his children laugh. Hamish sometimes watched from his window. Especially when he was missing his dad.

Hamish glanced at his own driveway. It was empty as usual. He felt a quick wave of sadness wash over him as he looked at the spot where his dad's car would once have been.

'I suppose I better get the dinner on!' said his mum, trying to keep things cheerful. She was only too aware how tough these last five months had been on the Ellerby family, ever since Boxing Day. 'Chips and beans and squash tonight! Go and tell Jimmy, will you, chicken?'

Jimmy was upstairs in his room as usual. He was listening to terrible music far too loudly.

'Jimmy?' said Hamish, standing at his door.

Jimmy sighed.

'My name is *James*?' he said, sniffily, like it was a question. 'And I would greatly appreciate it if this family would please refer to me as such?'

Hamish blinked at his brother. When had he become so pompous? Oh, that's right – when he turned fifteen.

'Sorry, Jimmy,' said Hamish. 'I mean, James?'

'Yes?' his brother said, all snippy. 'What is it? I'm very busy?'

Why did he always say everything like it was a question? And anyone could see he wasn't busy. Jimmy spent most of his time playing on his Xbox or trying to Skype with his girlfriend, lanky old Felicity Gobb. He'd go all soppy when he thought of her, like he was lost in a fog of Felicity Gobb. A Gobb-fog, Hamish called it. She always said everything like it was a question too, so Hamish actually preferred it when Jimmy and Felicity talked on Skype, because that meant she must be quite far away.

Sorry – I mean, *that must mean she must be quite far away?*

Also, whenever Felicity came round to the Ellerby house, she brought her little brother, Ratchett, and he was always burping and asking if he could take things home with him.

Like: 'Can I take this home with me?'

'No, Ratchett. That's our telly.'

Or: 'Can I take this home with me?'

'No, Ratchett. That's our Uncle Adrian.'

Or: 'Can I take this home with me?'

'Ratchett – you are literally pointing at our house.'

Didn't stop him trying, though. So Hamish was much happier when Felicity and Jimmy spoke on Skype.

'Mum says it's chips and beans tonight. Is that okay?' said Hamish.

Jimmy sighed heavily.

'Tell Mother I suppose if chips and beans *must* be forced upon me, I will bear it somehow?'

And then he slammed his door shut in Hamish's face and turned his music right up.

For a second, Hamish just stood there staring at the door. He and Jimmy used to do everything together. They'd get into adventures. They'd pretend the garden was a tropical island and they were dastardly pirates. They'd ride their bikes through the woods, acting like they were in a high-speed car chase. They were inseparable. And do you know what? In the old days, if Jimmy had found out Mole and Scratch were giving Hamish a hard time, he'd have stepped in like a proper big brother. He'd have stepped in like Captain Beetlebottom. And he'd have definitely wanted to help Hamish understand why the world seemed to keep stopping . . .

Now it was like Jimmy – I mean, *James* – didn't have time for Hamish at all. It was all just . . . *Gobb-fogs*. Mum said Jimmy was hurting. That he missed Dad as much as Hamish did. She said that maybe he was being distant because he didn't want to get hurt again. But Hamish still felt Jimmy had decided that his little brother was too young and immature to be interesting any more. And a small part of Hamish wondered that if he dealt with problems like Scratch Tuft and Mole Stunk himself then maybe Jimmy would be impressed. Maybe he'd even want to hang out with him again.

Hamish went into his own room and sat down on his bed. He stared at the sunflower on his windowsill. Even that made him think about his dad. He was the one who'd put it there in the first place and now Hamish looked after it carefully, helping it thrive and grow, even though his dad wasn't there to see it. How come everything had changed recently?

His mum was doing her best to look after them while also holding down her job and keeping things cheerful. She always made sure they got chips and beans, or little things that made them happy. Hamish knew she missed his dad too. Some nights he was sure he could hear her crying, but she'd never say anything in the morning and Hamish didn't feel brave enough to ask without upsetting her again.

There was one thing he could rely on to make him happy, though.

Hamish opened his bedside drawer and pulled out a small blue box. It had gold writing on it, which said: *The Explorer.* He flipped the box open.

There it was, inside. Glinting in the light. Still ticking. The Explorer. His dad's old watch. It never seemed to need winding up. But strangely, it always ran a bit fast. Hamish took good care of the watch. He would take it out of its box every day, give it a polish, correct the time and think of the day all those months ago his dad had given it to him.

Hamish's dad had been in sales. No one really knew what that meant. But he'd spent a lot of time away from Starkley, cruising down the motorways in the sleek Vauxhall Vectra his company had given him. He was always full of stories of magic and wonder when he returned, telling Hamish about amazing sounding places like 'Guild-fjord' or 'Croydonia'. These were places where it seemed like *anything* could happen! Hamish would get the Boggle set ready while his dad would tell him stories of checking into Travelodges or Holiday Inns near motorway service stations – only to find out he was being followed by a group of angry Romanian spies. Or he'd find strange alien life forms trying to steal the sausages from his room-service tray. Or he'd stumble across a gang of devious international body smugglers while trying to pay for his parking.

Hamish loved listening to his dad's adventures. They'd sit and play until bedtime and he'd listen and listen and listen.

Right up until that day when the Vauxhall hadn't come home.

Sometimes Hamish wondered if The Explorer had been a goodbye present. But he always stopped himself. After all, you give someone a goodbye present when you know you're going away, don't you? And his dad had just disappeared; he hadn't known he was leaving. He *couldn't* have left them on purpose.

'Hamish! Jimmy! Dinnertime!' shouted Hamish's mum from downstairs, shaking him from thoughts of his dad.

'It's JAMES?' shouted Jimmy, grumpily. 'Does ANYBODY

in this blinking house respect my name?'

'I forgot you were James now!' shouted his mum. 'Sorry, Jimmy!'

Hamish decided to wear his dad's watch to school tomorrow.

The Explorer would make him feel brave in the face of Scratch and Mole.

Almost without thinking, Hamish glanced out of the window, just in case tonight was the night he would finally see his dad's Vauxhall Vectra pulling back into their driveway. In case tonight was the night his dad finally came home.

4

Flash!

The next morning, Hamish had a lot on his mind.

The whole world-stopping thing was troubling him, but even more pressingly he had two rather angry girls expecting a very large delivery of Chomps.

Over breakfast he came up with a plan: all he had to do was avoid Scratch and Mole at all costs.

Hamish had worked out that to buy two million Chomp bars would mean saving his pocket money for 219 years. Either that or convincing his mum to sell their house and he wasn't sure how well she'd respond to that. So avoidance was the only way forward.

But if that failed, by raiding his old-age savings he'd managed to scrape together enough change to buy at least two Chomp bars. Hopefully, that would be enough to keep the ghastly, grubby girls off his back for a bit.

'Right!' yelled his mum, halfway out of the door. 'See you tonight!'

Hamish watched her hurry off down the driveway,

scribbling lipstick over her face while all manner of things fell out of her bag. Every time she stooped to pick one up, something else fell out of another pocket.

'Oops!' she said, as change clattered all around her and her paperwork threatened to blow away in the wind.

'Oops!' she said, chasing some coins down the street, accidentally squiggling her lipstick over her cheeks and then watching her papers fly off in the opposite direction.

Poor Mum, thought Hamish, setting off for school.

As he passed the sign outside the newsagent's advertising the *Starkley Post*, he took in the headline.

<u>MAN LEAVES TOWN</u>

That's weird, he thought. *It must be last week's paper.*

But no, Hamish was wrong. It was today's paper. The same story two weeks in a row? Well, that seems odd.

Winterbourne School was quite a modern school. It had low buildings with wide windows, and a big yellow sign saying 'Well, hello there!' to welcome people in. It was much nicer than St Autumnal's, down the road. That school looked like a big red prison, or somewhere wizards might go. The kids at St Autumnal were pretty stuck-up and the two schools didn't really mix much.

Outside the main door, Mr Longblather was talking to the headmistress, Frau Fussbundler. He was obviously being even more boring than usual, because she looked like a flower that was wilting in the rain. She kept saying things like 'Well, anyway,' and 'Goodness, look at the time,' but Mr Longblather didn't seem to get the hint and just kept *blah-blah-blah*-ing away.

The PE teacher, Tyrus Quinn, was doing squat thrusts outside the gym in a tracksuit that was a little too tight for him. For a PE teacher, he was remarkably tubby. Imagine if a cat tried to squeeze into one of your socks. That's how he looked in that tracksuit. Mr Quinn used to be one of Hamish's favourite teachers. But recently, he'd seemed a lot . . . meaner.

Talking of meanies, Hamish glanced nervously around. He couldn't see Scratch Tuft or Mole Stunk anywhere.

Usually, they'd be with Grenville in the corner of the playground, making menacing faces at the smaller kids. But today Grenville was alone, reading his wrestling magazine and practising his moves.

Hamish looked at his dad's watch. It was a bit too big for him, so he'd used rubber bands to stop it slipping off his wrist. It was almost nine o'clock now. If the school bell went on time at just after nine and Scratch and Mole hadn't shown up, he might just get away with it.

But then . . .

'OI! HAMISH ELLERBY!'

Oh no.

'C'MERE, YOU BULBOUS LITTLE PIPSQUEAK!'

There they were! Fresh off their little pink bikes and striding towards him. Hamish felt in his pocket for his chocolate bars, praying they would be enough.

'YOU WRETCHED LITTLE GRIZZLER, HAMISH!'

He began to walk backwards, away from them, but backed straight into the school fence. Now he had nowhere to go. All he could do was stand there and wait, as they got closer, and closer, and—

Wait.

What was *that*?

Was that a flash of lightning? Just a brief, quick flash from a faraway bolt?

Hamish looked up to the sky. It was grey, just like it usually was in Starkley, but it wasn't raining today. He listened for a roll of thunder . . .

Which is when he realised he could hear nothing at all.

Not a word.

Not a laugh.

Not a scream.

Not Tyrus Quinn grunting while he did his squat thrusts.

Not Grenville practising his moves.

Not Mr Longblather's blather.

It had all stopped with the flash.

Hamish looked around the playground.

Scratch and Mole were just a few metres away from him, angry looks on their furious little faces. Their fists were clumped into tight little balls. Their sharp, wonky, yellow teeth were bared. But they were still. Hamish waved his hand in front of their faces to see if they would move, but their tiny eyeballs just stared into nothingness.

Well, this could be interesting, he thought.

And, as he waved his hand some more, Hamish noticed his dad's watch rattling around on his wrist . . . It was still ticking.

He checked Scratch's watch. It had stopped.

He checked Mole's watch. It had stopped too.

But The Explorer kept going, kept ticking, kept *working*.

Something about this made him feel braver. It made him feel like he wasn't alone. He had his dad's watch here. Maybe that was a bit like having his dad.

Hamish had an idea. The Explorer had a stopwatch on it. He pressed Start and began to time the . . . well, what would you call it? The Pause? He began to time it and slowly started to walk around the playground . . .

A football was hanging way up off the ground. Two boys

had frozen in mid-air, trying to head it. Hamish walked right the way around them, checking in case there were any wires holding them up, still not convinced this wasn't some kind of trick or joke that the whole town was playing on him. He noticed a 5p coin was falling from the smaller boy's pocket. Hamish reached up and tucked it back in.

Astrid Carruthers was like a floating statue, jumping high above her skipping rope. Her face was frozen in a permanent grin.

Grenville Bile was holding Colin Robinson up and had obviously been about to chuck him in a bush. Poor Colin Robinson.

And look – a bee was about to sting a kid much smaller than Hamish. So very, very carefully, Hamish used two fingers to move the bee right the way to the other side of the playground.

And before he knew it—

The playground erupted into noise once more.

Tyrus Quinn kept grunting.

The two boys jumping for the ball bopped their heads together and fell to the ground, grouching and ouch-ing.

Astrid kept skipping.

Colin was flung into that bush.

The bee stung a tree.

And – oh my gosh! – Scratch and Mole kept running at where Hamish had been standing . . .

Except he wasn't standing there any more.

CRASH!

Scratch and Mole ran straight into the wire fence then bounced back and landed slap-bang on their bottoms.

'**Ooooooooow!**' they yelped. '**OoooooooW!**'

The whole playground filled with laughter as the girls hobbled away, clutching their bums. People used one hand to point and another to hold their aching sides.

Hamish pressed the Stop button on his stopwatch.

'Seven minutes and seven seconds,' he said, reading the watch face.

And then, quietly, he wondered what *else* you could do in seven minutes and seven seconds.

What Would You Do?

Scratch and Mole avoided Hamish for the rest of the day.

They were sore and humiliated. And they didn't understand how they could have been running at Hamish one second and flat on the floor the next. Their pride was hurt. How had stupid Hamish Ellerby outwitted them? They skulked around, eyeing him suspiciously. Every now and again they strolled up to their hero, Grenville Bile, and pointed at Hamish and whispered.

Grenville Bile just stared at him, cracking his knuckles.

But this whole thing had taught Hamish a lesson. He knew he had to be careful from now on. If the world stopped again and he wasn't back in position when it started, people would begin to notice. He had got away with it this time. But this was his secret. Only he and The Explorer seemed unaffected by the Flash. Only he and his Explorer could move around in the Pause.

But why? And what was he supposed to do? He couldn't

help but feel there must be a greater *purpose* to all this.

He just needed to work out what it was.

The last bell of the day rang and Hamish walked out of the classroom and into the long and squeaky corridor. He found himself next to his friend, Robin.

'Robin,' said Hamish, a little sheepishly. 'Can I ask you something?'

'Is it something I'll know the answer to?' replied Robin, nervously. 'Because if it's not, I'd rather you didn't.'

Robin was a nervous kid. And he didn't like to be asked anything he wasn't entirely sure of. The problem was, that was most things. For example, you couldn't ask him anything about maths, history or science.

Or English, French or geography.

And don't ask him about gardening.

Or tadpoles or space.

Or spinach.

Especially spinach.

Luckily, right now, Hamish didn't want to ask Robin anything about spinach.

'What would you do,' Hamish asked, making sure no one else was listening, 'if the whole world stopped still and you were the only thing that didn't?'

Robin raised two thick eyebrows as they made their way down the stairs towards the school doors.

'An interesting question, my friend,' he replied, in an important voice and putting both hands behind his back. 'I suppose . . . I'd mainly eat hamburgers and cheese.'

'Oh,' said Hamish.

'And I'd stay up really late. And then eat more hamburgers and cheese.'

Robin loved hamburgers and cheese. Though, strangely, he hated cheeseburgers.

'You'd stay up late and eat hamburgers?' said Hamish, a little disappointed. 'Is that it?' He was sure there had to be something better to do in the Pause than that.

'No,' said Robin. 'Of course not. I'd also watch telly. And I'd play all the games I'm not allowed to play, because they're PEGI 15. And I'd watch all the Rambo films, except for the bits where he's shooting guns, because I find all that a little unsettling. And then I'd go to the swimming pool and turn on the wave machine and practise my surfing.'

He stopped himself.

'Taking care,' Robin continued, 'to observe any and all safety procedures, of course . . .'

Hamish started to feel some excitement bubbling up in his tummy.

'I'd have such fun,' said Robin, actually getting quite into the idea now. 'But mainly I'd eat hamburgers and cheese.'

Hamish had a thought.

'But wouldn't you be scared?' he asked.

'Scared?' said Robin. '*Pah!* Scared of what?'

This was weird. Robin was scared of pretty much everything.

'Well . . . scared that the world wouldn't start again? I mean – that's a pretty scary thought, right?'

Robin started to laugh.

'Who cares! It would be a *world without rules*, Hamish! You could do whatever you wanted! No more bedtime, no more schooltime, no more having-to-get-up-when-your-mum-tells-you time!'

'I see . . .' said Hamish, realising Robin had a point. And if Robin wasn't scared, why should Hamish be?

'No more eating your five-a-day!' said Robin, with glee. 'No more making sure you drink enough water! You could have a Fanta bath! You could cook spaghetti and Maltesers for breakfast! You'd never have to do a squat thrust again! You could do whatever you wanted, because the *whole world would be yours*, Hamish!'

Hamish looked at Robin. His eyes were shining from the sheer delight of it all. Then he shook his head and came back to earth.

'Of course,' he said, pushing open the doors of the school and starting to skip down the steps to the playground. 'In real life it would be awful.'

'Would it?'

'Oh, yes. It would be terrifying. I'd hate it. But as an idea . . .' But Hamish had stopped listening, because he had noticed a police car at the school gates. Its light was flashing and standing in front of it were two stern officers in uniform. The kids streaming out of the gates all slowed as they saw them. The officers were staring at the crowd, obviously looking for someone.

Hamish felt immediately guilty.

Oh, no, he thought. *It's me. They're after me. They're going to arrest me, because the world stopped and I kept moving around.* This was it. This was the moment Hamish Ellerby would be arrested and sent to a home for malevalunt kids!

I mean malovelant.

Oh, you know what I mean.

But . . .

'Scratch Tuft and Mole Stunk?' said the first policewoman.

Slowly, the crowd parted. Scratch and Mole stood together, in the centre. They reached out to find each other's hand. Hamish realised that no matter how fierce and foul they could be, they were still just little girls.

'I'm afraid I have some bad news about your parents,' said the police officer, gently, and as they began to tremble, she led them quietly away.

MADAME COUS COUS'S
INTERNATIONAL WORLD OF TREATS

What Robin said had really made Hamish think.

If the world kept stopping – but *he* didn't – well, imagine all the amazing things he could do. He was getting extra time, after all. If the next Pause lasted for the same time as the one earlier, he'd get at least *seven minutes and seven seconds* of extra time! Hamish felt certain that with enough of these Pauses, he could do something really worthwhile. He could invent something, perhaps, like a flying car or a hover spoon. Or he could come up with a cure for all known diseases. Or he could work to bring peace to the world.

He *could* do all of that.

Or he could just eat loads of sweets.

That would be quite a good short-term plan while he worked out the finer details, Hamish decided, and just to make a head start on that plan, he turned in the direction of the high street.

Hamish pushed open the door of Madame Cous Cous's International World of Treats. The little bell above the door tinkled.

The sunlight was streaming through big square windows, but that wasn't dust dancing in the air. It was sugar.

Madame Cous Cous did not look up when she heard the bell. She was perched behind the counter, reading the *Starkley Post* and eating cocktail sausages from a mug.

Oh, Hamish loved this place! All the kids in Starkley did. Madame Cous Cous stocked the finest sweets and candies from across the globe. The shop was legendary. One of the few places in town you could definitely *not* call boring. Dad used to bring him here all the time, calling it their 'secret mission', and buy him whatever he liked. It was the only reason Hamish had needed a filling from Dr Fussbundler. He rubbed his cheek and winced at the thought of that enormous dentist's drill. The way it juddered and shuddered into his poor tooth until he could feel his brain rattling about in his head. But it was worth every second, he decided, if it meant he could still go into Madame Cous Cous's.

Once a year, this unusual old lady would book a round-the-world ticket and set off on a month-long adventure.

She'd take trains, and planes, and buses, bikes and unicycles.

She'd climb mountains and swim rivers.

She'd fight bears and squish spiders!

And all because she was determined to bring the very best treats from around the world to the children of Starkley.

In France, she discovered the sweetest, most delicate cheese-and-bacon-flavoured mints sold by a glum old gum farmer high up in the Pyrenees mountains. She brought that stuff back to Starkley and it sold out within the hour! *Délicieux!*

In Italy, she wrestled with the Italian Prime Minister for the last box of Italian candied prawns. He thought he should get them just because he was prime minister. Well, Madame Cous Cous wasn't having that. So she grappled him out of the shop, and into the narrow streets outside, and down an alleyway, and into a gondola, which she then used to row all the way to the airport with that box of candied prawns under one arm. DELIZIOSO!

She sold Mexican chilli sherbet. **ÑAM!**

She sold peanut butter eggs she found high up in a Russian tree. **VKUSSNY!**

She sold American fried jelly. **DEEE-LISH!**

And those enormous toffee sausages everyone walks about with in Germany. **Super-schmackhaft!**

The only thing she didn't sell was Norwegian salted gobstoppers. She simply could not stand those Norwegian tongue girdlers. They offended her so much, in fact, that she had banned *all* Norwegians from her shop.

So, because she wanted the kids of Starkley to have (almost) all the sweets of the world, you might imagine Madame Cous Cous was quite a lovely woman. And she was . . .

Until the day she wasn't.

She had returned in February from her month-long trip away with absolutely *no* new sweets. Just a packet of Tic Tacs she bought at the airport. Her cloud of white hair, which had once been so soft and thick, was now a dark grey – like each and every hair was suddenly in a bad mood. Her once rosy cheeks seemed to have spread – so that now her whole face was a particularly angry red. And whenever anyone asked her what had happened to make her this way, she would bark at them, like a very fierce dog.

It was rather odd to see a grown woman barking like a dog.

Many people wondered whether she'd been swapped for her own evil twin – that was how bad and mean she'd become.

Now Madame Cous Cous even kept a gnarled brown stick behind her counter with which she'd hit children if they took too long to get their change out. It wasn't even *their* fault they took so long – their poor little hands were shaking, because they knew this fearsome OAP would rap their knuckles or thwack their backsides with that big long stick like it was nothing at all. Some kids would spend all evening picking splinters out of their bottoms after a visit to Madame Cous Cous.

Which meant that Hamish now approached the counter with caution.

Underneath a large white sign that said

ONLY ONE-AND-A-QUARTER SCHOOLCHILDREN AT A TIME!

Madame Cous Cous looked up at him, bored.

'Yeeees?' she said.

'Um . . .' said Hamish, trying to decide what sweet to ask for.

'What do you mean, "Um . . ."?' said Madame Cous Cous, slamming her fist down on the desk with such force that an entire bottle of Brazilian Banana Babies shook on the shelf.

'WHAT DOES THAT BIG RED SIGN SAY?'

Hamish looked up at it.

'It s-s-s-says "No Norwegians",' he stuttered.

Madame Cous Cous closed her eyes, furious.

'**NOT THAT BIG RED SIGN!**' she yelled. '**THE OTHER ONE!**'

Hamish read the sign next to it.

'Well . . . that one says "COMPLETE SILENCE".'

'**EXACTLY!**' she shrieked, pointing one skinny finger at him. 'And **YOU** just **SPOKE!**'

'But . . . but you asked me a question!' said Hamish, desperately. 'You said "yeeees?"'

'**SO WHAT?**' she said, bringing her big stick out. 'You didn't have to **ANSWER!** You could have performed a small mime!'

'A *mime*?' said Hamish.

'**STOP TALKING!**' she yelled. '**I WANT COMPLETE SILENCE!** Did I not make that **CLEAR?**'

'Yes,' said Hamish. 'But you keep asking—'

'Will you **STOP TALKING!**' she shouted.

'I'm sorry,' said Hamish, confused. 'I honestly didn't mean to—'

'*Right!* That's it!' said Madame Cous Cous, one snooty

nose in the air. 'You are **BANNED!**'

'Banned?' said Hamish, and then he realised he'd said it out loud and quickly covered his mouth with both hands.

'Banned!' she said. 'The ratty little motormouth Hamish Ellerby is **BANNED** from Madame Cous Cous's International World of Treats and so are **ALL HIS FRIENDS FOREVER!**'

She wrote his name down in her ledger and finished with a flourish. This was awful! This was dreadful! Why was she doing this?

'No Polish Butter Lollies for you!' she said, with a foul and twisted smile, leaning in close to Hamish's face so he could see it properly. 'No Afghan Aniseed! No Belgian Bon Bons! No Swedish Cinnamons! No Chinese Wispas!'

Hamish started to back out of the shop, as Madame Cous Cous seemed to grow bigger and bigger and get angrier and angrier.

Hamish could see that the door to the stockroom was slightly open. There were boxes and boxes of unopened Chomps in there. There must have been *millions!*

'No Edinburgh Eye Poppers for you!' she cried. 'No Falaraki FizzWizzers! Nothing at all for you *or* your friends **– FOREVER!**'

And then she began to bark. And Hamish turned and ran out of the shop.

All Hamish could hear as he sprinted down the road was the cackle of Madame Cous Cous – gatekeeper of the sweets – and the howl of what sounded like a mad dog in quite some pain.

When Hamish got home, he found his mum on the phone, looking very worried.

She still had lipstick all over her face from this morning.

'Poor Scratch and Mole,' she said, putting the handset down. 'Such lovely little girls.'

Hamish scrunched his nose up. Lots of grown-ups seemed to think Scratch and Mole were very polite and well-spoken. They didn't realise they behaved like completely different children in front of other people's parents.

Instead of growling things like, **'C'MERE, YOU WINKLE-FACED NINNYHAMMER!'** they'd say things like, 'Oh, Mrs Ellerby, you *do* look lovely today', or, 'My, what a wonderful morning it is. How *lucky* we are to be alive!'.

I bet you do that too, you little stink nit.

'What happened, Mum?' asked Hamish. 'I saw the police at school.'

She sat him down.

'Their parents . . . well, they seem to have disappeared.'

'What – all four of them?' said Hamish. 'At once?'

'Yes,' said his mum. 'It's the strangest thing. Someone thinks they probably went on holiday to Magaluf and just decided to let the girls look after themselves. What a terrible, terrible thing.'

Hamish thought of his own missing dad, and his mum could see it.

'Oh, Hamish,' she said. 'I know. We . . .'

But she didn't know what to say. What *could* she say?

She'd *usually* just say, 'We have to just carry on.'

'That's okay, Mum,' said Hamish, not wanting to have that conversation. 'I'm going to go and get changed and then I said I'd meet up with Robin.'

Hamish's mum looked at him sadly. Hamish turned away before she tried to talk to him about it again.

'Have you noticed something weird going on with the grown-ups?' said Hamish, sitting on his favourite swing at the park. He'd changed into his after-school clothes – his white jumper with the big blue 'H' on, his black and white baseball shoes with the silver wings and his cool black jeans.

'What do you mean?' asked Robin, who had his binoculars out, because he thought he'd seen a worm at the other end of the park. Robin was absolutely terrified of worms. That was why he always wore wellington boots.

'It just feels like there's something weird going on,' said Hamish. 'Like how come Madame Cous Cous is so horrible now?'

'Oh,' said Robin, still on the lookout for evil worms. 'That place is scary. I don't go in there any more.'

'Well, that's lucky,' said Hamish. 'Because you're banned.'

'I'm what?' said Robin, looking at Hamish in shock.

'You're banned for life. All my friends are, because I spoke out loud.'

Robin sighed.

'Well, that's a relief really,' he said. 'Last time it took me a week to get all the splinters out of my bottom from her bashing stick. But yes, I've noticed some grown-ups are a lot grumpier than they used to be.'

'Like who?'

'Like Rex Ox at school,' he said. 'He had his leaf blower out the other day. You know how I hate loud noises. Well, when he saw my football, he stuck it right on the end and then blew it way up into the sky. It went up and up for ages.

He just kept laughing. I think my ball's probably on Mars by now.'

Hamish was shocked. Rex Ox had always been a great caretaker. He used to let the kids steer the school's ride-on lawnmower. And the only reason he'd stopped was because Manjit Singhdaliwal had completely lost control one day and ended up carving his own name into the school field by accident. The *Starkley Post* said there were only two man-made things an astronaut could see from the moon: the Great Wall of China, and the name Manjit Singhdaliwal scribbled in ginormous letters on a field in Starkley. But Rex Ox took the blame for that, just like he did when some of the kids tried to make a parachute by sellotaping all the umbrellas from Lost Property together. They didn't realise it would catch the wind before they had a chance to try it. Twelve kids ended up stuck up a lamp post four miles away in Frinkton. It was Rex Ox that got them down and kept the whole thing quiet. He had always been a caretaker who *took care* of things, which made Robin's story very confusing.

'Why on earth would Rex Ox suddenly use his leaf blower for evil?' asked Hamish.

Robin shrugged.

'He said he did it just because he could.'

Hamish was amazed. But, now he thought about it, Robin was right. Rex Ox *had* been a lot grumpier recently. And then there was Tyrus Quinn. Ever since he'd gone on a weekend away to Bruges, he'd been in a foul mood. Sometimes he'd make the kids do cross-country runs in their pants – even when it wasn't PE! He'd just stroll into a science lesson and shout, 'Right, you horrible bunch of abominable oddballs! Start running!' And then he'd blow a whistle and chase them out of the school and into the woods, waving his stopwatch while they screamed.

And then there was Grenville Bile's mum.

Oh, Mrs Bile was the worst. Because she had been grumpy for AGES! Well, with everyone except her pampered little darling Grenville, anyway. Now she was like *double-* horrible.

Hamish did a very good job of avoiding Grenville Bile and his mum – the woman they called the Postmaster.

'I heard all the grumpiness is to do with the economy,' said Robin. 'That's what my sister told me.'

'What does that mean?'

'I have absolutely no idea,' he replied.

Hmm. Well, maybe the economy was something Hamish could sort out in the next Pause. Surely seven minutes and seven seconds would be enough for something like that?

Briefly he thought about telling Robin about what had been happening. It felt like too big a secret to keep to himself . . . but this was a kid who was scared of *worms*. And leaf blowers. And sudden noises. And Velcro. Once, Hamish jokingly told him that the Wizard of Oz was based on a true story and Robin hadn't left the house for a week. Hamish couldn't imagine what would happen if he told him the *whole world* was stopping!

'It's a shame about Madame Cous Cous,' said Robin, before Hamish could say anything anyway. 'I promised my mum I'd buy her some Japanese Jellied Fish-Shavings for her birthday. Now I suppose I'll have to go all the way to Japan to get some.'

Or maybe, thought Hamish, *there was another way*.

All he needed now was for the world to stop.

7

Here We Go!

The next day, Hamish knew one thing: he was ready for a Pause.

He had it all worked out. He had his Explorer. So he would explore.

He also made sure he had some chalk with him. He knew having some chalk with him would be very important. He could use it for all sorts of things. Drawing arrows. Marking spots. Did you know that a line of chalk can stop ants in their tracks? It's absolutely true. Did you know a little chalk can get grease out of your clothes? That's true too. Did you know that if you start to *lick* a stick of chalk . . . people will think you're an absolute weirdo? That's the truest of the lot. Anyway, the point is Hamish knew that chalk could be *really* useful for adventures.

As he got dressed, Hamish kept one eye on the world outside. The trees were swaying. The breeze was blowing. But he knew it could all stop at any moment. That was the really exciting thing.

He waited all through breakfast and flinched every time he thought he saw a flash.

But it was always just Jimmy taking selfies in the kitchen.

He waited on the walk to school . . . and he kept waiting during assembly . . . and his first lesson . . . and his second lesson . . . and his breaktime . . . and his lunchtime . . . and he waited as he trudged all the way home again.

But the world did not stop.

The day after that, Hamish *knew* he was really ready. If anything, the day before had just been a dress rehearsal.

As well as his chalk, he'd also found a silver whistle he thought might come in handy, and a keyring with a torch on it. You never knew when you'd need a keyring with a torch on it.

Once again, he waited as he got ready for school.

And he waited all through breakfast.

He waited on the walk to school and he waited *all day long*.

But nothing happened. Nothing at all. The world just kept on going.

Hamish started to wonder . . . had he missed his chance?

What if the world just wasn't going to Pause again?

And then it was Saturday, which was normally the best day of all. Despite that, Hamish was pretty down in the dumps.

Why isn't the world stopping any more? he thought, as he plodded towards the high street.

Starkley High Street had all the usual things. There was the sweet shop, of course, the butcher's, a small supermarket run by a funny little man in a sailor's cap and the newsagent's. There was Slackjaw's Motors too, which always had a fleet of brilliant blue Vespas out the front. Hamish had lost count of the number of times he would just stop and stare at those cool little scooters each week. His dad had told him he used to drive around on one when he was a teenager and Hamish thought that was the greatest thing ever. He couldn't wait until he was a teenager, because then maybe he could drive about on one too. He couldn't understand why Jimmy wasted the fact he was old enough to do cool things like that and instead just wanted to speak to Felicity Gobb all day! Hamish had found one of Jimmy's love poems the other day.

It went:

FELICITY GOBB IS A GIRL THAT I LIKE?
MORE THAN A TRAIN AND
MORE THAN MY BIKE?
OH, FELICITY GOBB, HOW I LOVE THEE?
MORE THAN MY NOSE, BUT
NOT AS MUCH AS MY KNEE?

Turns out Jimmy wasn't very good at poetry.

Bleeurgh!

Anyway, Hamish thought as he crossed the road, *girls are one thing but Vespas are quite another, and if you had a Vespa, you—*

Hamish stopped dead in his tracks and held his breath.

Was that it? Was that a Flash?

He listened closely. The silence was overwhelming. It was in every nook and cranny. It was in every corner of every corner. It was like somehow the sound of nothing was louder than the sound of anything he'd ever heard before.

He glanced around, quite carefully. This was a Pause all right!

Everyone was still. Right in the middle of the street. Right in the middle of thoughts and conversations and ideas. Astrid Carruthers was halfway through some bubblegum. Her face was almost hidden by the pale-pink bubble billowing out of her mouth.

There were people walking out of shops, people walking into shops, people halfway through sitting down on benches. Hamish had once read about a place called Pompeii, where a big volcano had gone off, turning everybody to lava statues. And he'd heard about a Chinese Emperor who wanted some soldiers to protect him in the afterlife, so had thousands of fake ones created for him out of clay. This was like that – but with living, breathing people!

He would fit in as much as he could to this Pause, he decided. And there was something he should do for Robin too. He took out his Explorer and set the alarm for six and a half minutes. Assuming the Pause was the same length as the last one, that would give him more than enough time to explore and get back to the same spot before the world started again. Then he took out the chalk from his pocket and drew around his feet, marking where he'd been standing when the Flash had happened, so he could get back to it and no one would think he'd even moved.

He took a careful step forward and poked Astrid Carruthers in the arm.

Nothing. No response. Could she still feel that, he wondered? Would it hurt when she Unpaused?

Slowly, it started to hit him. *The world belonged to Hamish Ellerby.* He was the King of Everything! Whatever he wanted to do, he could do. Whatever he wanted to see, he could see.

But what was first? What had he always wanted to do?

Which is when he had an idea.

He turned around and saw it.

It looked *amazing*.

Could he?

No, surely not.

No, he couldn't.

Could he?

Hamish revved the sky-blue Vespa, feeling like the naughtiest kid in the world.

He also felt *cool*.

He knew how to ride one, because he'd looked it up on

YouTube once and it seemed easy enough. But he was only ten! There was no *way* he'd be allowed to do this with grown-ups watching!

He turned the handle and the mighty Vespa shot forward, leaving poor old Mr Slackjaw standing frozen behind him.

He'd been about to hand over the keys to someone for a test drive, but now his hand was empty. *I better remember to put the keys back*, Hamish thought, as he clung on.

Through town he rode, swerving in between pedestrians and weaving around bollards. He was mounting pavements and creating wind where there wasn't any. He shot past elderly Mr Picklelips so quickly the old man's hat blew clean off. Hamish would normally have gone and picked it up again, but time was of the essence! He probably only had four or five minutes left!

Round the roundabout by the bakery he went, again and again.

'Yahoooooo!' and the high-pitched *BVVVVVVT* of the scooter were now the only sounds in Starkley.

Hamish had never felt so free!

Up Lilyturf Street he sped – where he noticed Grenville Bile had one hand round a smaller kid's neck, and the other halfway up his nose as usual.

Down Alumroot Alley he motored and went past the Queen's Leg pub. He swerved to avoid a cat on the road and caught his front wheel on the kerb.

Now he was doing a wheelie! He hadn't meant to, and he didn't particularly want to, but he was doing one! Imagine if his mum saw him now! She'd be livid!

He roared back to the high street, and then skidded to a stop.

He looked up at the sign.

MADAME COUS COUS'S
INTERNATIONAL WORLD OF TREATS

Hamish's tummy did a little double-flip as he clambered off the bike.

He was banned from the shop, he knew that. But this wasn't normal Starkley any more. There were no rules in the Pause.

But was there time? Could he risk it? He checked his watch. *Three minutes to go . . .*

Hamish crept inside. Madame Cous Cous seemed to be in the middle of a sneeze. She was holding her handkerchief, ready to catch it. Hamish could almost make out each and every individual germ that was headed for that grubby old thing, stuck still in the afternoon air.

Right, he thought. *Japanese Jellied Fish-Shavings for Robin and his mum.*

Robin's mum was very sweet, but, just like her son, she was nervous about everything. She still made Robin sit in a booster seat in the back of their brown Volvo and wear a helmet for any car journey, even if it was just to the shops. And she always made Robin tuck his trouser legs into his socks when going up or down stairs, because 'trouser legs are a real tripping hazard'. If Hamish was honest, he found it a bit annoying. But, after Hamish's dad had disappeared, she'd prepared all sorts of bean casseroles and mango curries and brought them round so that Hamish's mum didn't have to cook for a while. The last thing Hamish wanted was to be responsible for denying such a nice woman some disgusting-sounding candied fish product.

But just look at all those sweets!

Hamish licked his lips. Surely the angry old nit Madame Cous Cous wouldn't notice if a couple of Korean Caramels disappeared? Maybe just three or four? Or six or seven?

Hamish ran his fingers over the glass bottles on the lowest shelf. His mouth began to water at the sight of a Swiss Swizzler.

Slowly, he screwed open a jar and poked one little hand in.

But, as his fingers found a Swizzler, he caught sight of a small sign, right above Madame Cous Cous's head, reading:

THEFT IS THEFT!

Hamish's cheeks began to burn.

Feeling guilty, he immediately let the Swizzler drop back down.

This was wrong. This was taking something wonderful like the Pause and doing bad with it. He shouldn't be using it to his own advantage.

But what about Robin?

He'd got Robin banned from this place, so the least he could do was make sure he didn't have to go all the way to Tokyo for his mum's birthday present.

Then he glanced at the boxes of Chomps in the storeroom. Scratch and Mole would like some of those. Maybe he could take a couple for them. It might really cheer them up. Because, no matter how horrible they'd been to him recently, he knew what it was like when a parent disappeared.

And maybe he could just have a lick of a jam lolly while he was here. Who would begrudge a brave Pause traveller a lick of a jam lolly?

Hamish decided he would leave whatever money he had on the counter and write an IOU for the rest. He was pretty sure he had 20p in his pocket somewhere.

Unfortunately, it was at this point that Hamish realised that he couldn't put his hand in his pocket.

Because his hand was completely and utterly stuck in the bottle.

Oh, no.

Oh, goodness me, no!

Hamish tugged at his hand, but it wasn't budging. It was stuck fast! It was The Explorer! It was too chunky to get back out again!

He began to panic. How much time did he have left?

Hamish pulled and pulled at his hand.

'Come on!' he shouted. 'Come on!'

But his hand wouldn't budge. Not an inch. Not a squinch. Not a squiddly-dinch.

This was bad. This was awful. If the Pause ended and Madame Cous Cous caught Hamish like this, what on earth would she do? How would he explain suddenly appearing in her shop with his hand stuck in a jar of sweets? And so, with growing terror, he pulled, and he pulled, and he squeezed at his wrist, and finally . . .

. . . the glass bottle SHOT off his hand with the mightiest **POP!** and flew through the air. It bounced off a shelf and knocked all the other glass bottles to the floor with a *SMASH* and a **CRASH!** It landed on another shelf and knocked all those bottles off too! Bottle after bottle of strange and unusual sweets **CLATTERED** to the ground. Dundee Drizzle Balls rolled all over the place, bashing into Italian Candied Prawns. A bag of Mexican Chilli Sherbet fell to the floor and went off like an enormous smoke bomb.

And Madame Cous Cous just stood there, in the middle of her sneeze, like nothing was happening at all.

The place was an utter, frightful, dreadful, awe-inspiring MESS!

And then . . .

BEEP BEEP BEEP BEEP BEEP!

The Explorer's alarm was going off!

The world was about to start again! He had to go!

'I'm sorry, Madame Cous Cous!' Hamish shouted. 'I'm so sorry!'

And out of the shop he ran, grabbing a small bag of Japanese Jellied Fish-Shavings that was lying on top of the mess as he went. At least his first Pause exploration hadn't been a *complete* disaster! He jumped back on the scooter and swung it around. At a million miles an hour he raced back down the high street to Slackjaw's Motors, bouncing over speed bumps and clanking back to the ground. He jumped off the bike, took the keys out and shoved them back in Mr Slackjaw's hand.

He ran back to his position in front of the town clock and put his feet in the chalk-marks.

He'd done it!

He was back in place just as the world was about to start again!

Right now!

. . .

Any second . . . now!

. . .

Okay, not then . . . but *now*!

. . .

. . . Now?

But nothing changed at all.

Hamish caught his breath and glanced quickly at his watch. What?

Seven minutes and nineteen seconds.

Seven minutes and twenty seconds.

Had he got it wrong? Was the stopwatch broken?

It was then he heard something else. Something he had not noticed before. A bigger, deeper, louder tick . . . tick . . . tick.

The town clock above him was still working. It showed exactly the same time as The Explorer. So the town clock was not affected by the

Pause either. *That's why it always seems to run fast*, Hamish thought, because, just like The Explorer, the Starkley clock kept going when all the other clocks stopped!

Hamish started to sweat. Why wasn't the world starting again?

He waited and waited.

Eight minutes and twenty-six seconds.

Eight minutes and twenty-seven seconds . . . twenty-eight . . . twenty-nine . . .

Had he broken the world, like he'd broken the sweet shop?

And then Hamish spotted something.

A blackbird, just like the one he'd seen in his garden that night.

Its wings were spread and it was just centimetres from a shop window. Its little face looked scared. The world had stopped just as the bird was about to smash into the glass. That poor little guy – he would never survive when everything started again.

Eight minutes and thirty-five seconds.

What could Hamish do? Could he save the bird? What if the world started again before he'd done it?

Hamish knew he had to act fast. So he dashed away from the safety of his chalk footprints. He ran to the butcher's across the road – they had the stepladder out so they could wash the windows.

Eight minutes and forty-six seconds.

Hamish dragged the ladder to underneath the blackbird and he quickly clambered up, then gently turned the bird around so it was facing away from the window. He tenderly stroked its neck, just once, then checked The Explorer.

Eight minutes and fifty-nine seconds . . .

Things could Unpause at any moment. Hamish had to get back into position! He left the ladder where it was and ran straight back to his chalk footprints.

Nine minutes and seven seconds.

Nine minutes and eight seconds.

Nine minutes and nine seconds . . .

The world began again.

Cars. Cats. People.

'OOOH!' he heard, as Astrid's bubblegum popped.

'AAAATCHOOOO!' he heard, from the sweet shop down the road.

CLABANG! he heard, as the exhaust pipe fell off the Vespa and rolled around on the ground. Mr Slackjaw rubbed his head in confusion as the man who was about to buy it put his hands on his hips and walked away.

'OI! WHO'S NICKED MY LADDER?' yelled the butcher.

'Windy today, Hamish!' said old Mr Picklelips, putting his hat back on his head.

But Hamish didn't reply.

All he could think was that the Pause was getting longer. *Nine minutes and nine seconds.* What did that *mean*?

Just then, Madame Cous Cous ran out of her shop, waving her stick and holding her bright red face in one hand.

'I SNEEZED and all my blimmin' **SWEETS** fell over!' she barked, mad as a dog.

And somewhere far above that blackbird flapped away, safe.

It turned its head just once as it disappeared into the distance and only to look at Hamish.

ϺϺ

Hamish could hardly sleep that night.

His head was too full of possibilities.

How. Awesome. Was. This!

If the Pause was getting longer then one day it might be long enough for him to have some real fun. Anything-he-liked fun!

He could jump in a Ferrari and drive it all the way to Paris without anyone stopping him to ask why a ten-year-old was driving a Ferrari or where his passport was!

He could learn how to fly a helicopter and take a tour of the Grand Canyon! He could slip inside Buckingham Palace! He could tickle the Pope!

He could wander about in London Zoo and climb inside the cages with the animals! He could see whatever he wanted – China! Singapore! Liechtenstein!

He could build a giant chocolate egg and spend a whole day eating his way out of it!

Okay, that one was a bit weird, but the point is, Hamish could do anything he wanted if the Pauses lasted long enough. The world was *brilliant*. He needed to make plans!

Unfortunately, little did he know it . . . but, somewhere across town, someone had it in for poor old Hamish Ellerby.

And that someone had plans of his own.

8

Oh, No,
It's Grenville Bile!

It is time we talked about Grenville Bile.

To be honest, I've been putting it off for as long as possible, because no one really wants to talk about Grenville Bile. But he's about to play a bigger role in Hamish's life, so let's just bite the Bile bullet.

Deep down, like all bullies, Grenville Bilious Bile was lonely.

He had no brothers or sisters. His dad was quiet as a mouse and spent most of his days reading the paper in the Queen's Leg, trying to keep out of the way of Grenville's mum, the Postmaster.

The rumour was Mrs Bile hadn't always been fearsome. Some of the grown-ups claimed they could remember when she seemed quite a kindly soul, organising raffles to raise money for new school footballs, or making sandwiches for old people who'd already eaten.

That certainly wasn't the case any more.

Tubitha Bile was *awful*.

Hamish had noticed that every single weekend of the year so far, Grenville had been trailing after his mother and doing all the chores she couldn't be bothered with.

Like:

- Polishing her peanuts so that each one was as smooth and peanutty as possible.

- Using a very tiny comb to brush all the wiry hair on her moles.

And worst of all . . .

- Degreasing the chairs where her oily, boily bottom had been.

But Grenville was *greatly* rewarded for such tireless work. He would always show off about all the things his mum had bought him. All you had to do was mention a new toy you had and up he'd pop, from behind a bush, to say: 'Yeah? Well, I've got the *whole set* at home!'

Grenville had the whole set of Super Action Rascals.

He was allowed to download any film he wanted.

He had all the latest video games, even the ones you had to be eighteen to play. He had every single football kit of every single football club in the land. He had a PlayStation, an Xbox, an iPad, a laptop, six walkie-talkies, two radio-controlled cars and a life-sized model of a raccoon. Grenville certainly seemed to have it all. But would he share any of it? Not on your nelly. And no one ever went round to his house to play with any of it either. Not even Robin, who *loved* raccoons.

The Postmaster was very firm:

NO KIDS ALLOWED.

Everyone in Starkley feared the Postmaster. It wasn't just the way she lunked around, scowling at everybody. Nor was it her deep, gargly voice, or the way she tossed her cigar butts at cats.

No. People were scared of her, because she was the

gatekeeper to the post office – and she ran it exactly as she pleased.

The Postmaster had no time for other people's rules. It was down to how she was feeling as to whether or not you got your post every day. Which meant that she decided whether you got your birthday money from your Auntie Freda, or that parcel from your grandma in Australia, or anything anyone sent you at all.

If she decided to be kind, you might – *might!* – get your presents.

But if she'd seen you walking too close to her car, or throwing sticks at a tree to get your frisbee out, or pulling your sister's hair, or standing on a chair to reach the biscuits your mum puts in the very top cupboard . . . then forget about it. You'll never see those presents. They'll mysteriously disappear. **'LOST IN THE POST!'** she'll shout at your mum and dad, slamming down the iron grill and retreating to the cup of coffee that's turned her teeth dark brown all these years.

(Incidentally, the Postmaster makes a lot of money selling things on eBay, although no one knows where she gets all that stuff from.)

Even the grown-ups of Starkley would find their post was

'lost' if they angered her. Poor old Mr Picklelips hadn't had a letter since Christmas, and all because his nose sometimes did a little whistle the Postmaster found annoying.

Well, all this had quite an effect on Grenville.

His mum's bad moods transferred straight to him. And so did a lot of her power in town. People didn't want to annoy Grenville for fear of annoying the Postmaster and this made him feel *untouchable*.

The butcher gave him free sausages.

The funny little man in the supermarket let him choose any comics he wanted.

Madame Cous Cous never once hit him with a stick.

He was allowed to wear his Mexican wrestling mask to school any time he liked.

And Scratch and Mole would do anything he asked of them.

And that, of course, was the problem. Now that Scratch and Mole were off school, Grenville found himself lonelier than ever.

Maybe that makes you feel sorry for him.

Well, don't! Stop that right now!

Grenville Bile is the biggest jackwagon in Starkley! Thundering about the place in his 'Too Cool For School'

T-shirt, knocking over bins and switching signs around so that people who want to go to the supermarket end up in the swimming pool and people who want to go to the swimming pool end up walking around the supermarket in their swimming trunks!

But, like a gangster without any 'associates' to distract him, Grenville was bored.

Before the girls had gone, they'd told him that Hamish had knocked them over. They were running at him, they said, and he managed to get behind them. They had no idea how. They said they thought he was magic.

Grenville didn't believe in magic. And he didn't appreciate his associates being disrespected.

You don't disrespect associates of Grenville Bile.

He knew he had to put Hamish *Smell*erby back in his place.

The Terrible News

Well, I'm glad we got that over with. Let's get back to Hamish, eh?

For the last twenty-four hours, Hamish had been working on his Pause Survival Kit (or PSK as he'd decided to call it).

Right now it was all kept in a long metal tin of chocolate Mustn'tgrumbles his mum had finished.

And inside . . .

ONE CHOMP

ONE PIECE OF CHALK (GREEN)

ONE BOTTLE OF WATER (SMALL)

PLASTERS

ONE KEYRING WITH TORCH ATTACHMENT.

ONE SILVER WHISTLE

ANOTHER CHOMP (JUST IN CASE

He had decided to keep his PSK at the bottom of his schoolbag until the next Pause. And he'd make sure he was always wearing The Explorer.

He knew it was so important to be ready. But he also knew that, since all the chaos he'd accidentally caused during the last Pause, he had to be careful. He couldn't change too much about the world while it had stopped, because people would begin to really notice. The whole town would start to question what was going on – and Hamish didn't want to spoil things. Something magic was happening in Starkley and for some reason he was right at the centre of it.

If his dad was around, he'd have told him all about the Pause. His dad always had time for him. They'd spend those long evenings playing Boggle and talking about all his many adventures. If anyone knew what was going on with the Pause, Hamish reckoned it would be his dad. As great as Mum and Jimmy were, there was nothing quite like talking to Dad.

The night his dad hadn't come home – the night of Boxing Day – Hamish had still thought it was all going to be okay. His dad had only popped out to buy crisps and a tub of ice cream, because *Star Wars* was on and he said he wanted the boys to watch it with him. No one had batted an eyelid when he hadn't come back an hour later.

'He must have bumped into someone,' said Hamish's mum, nodding to herself.

But then it was two hours.

And then the film started.

'You keep watching, chickens,' said Hamish's mum, getting up to go to the kitchen, where she rang Dad's mobile over and over and over again.

Hamish had stayed up for hours that night, with his face pressed against the window.

No one ever found Dad's car. He'd simply vanished.

Hamish thought again of the police that had arrived at school to fetch Scratch and Mole. The police had come to *his* house on Boxing Day evening too and he remembered the endless phone calls his mum had made to anyone who might know anything at all. For days afterwards, Hamish had cycled round Starkley on his bike, checking every alleyway and looking through as many windows as he could, just in case.

Mum was right about Jimmy too. He had just closed up that night. He'd stopped wanting to hang out with Hamish as much. He didn't want to play two-player games on the Xbox any more. He didn't want to play with any of the

Christmas presents he'd got. Jimmy seemed to just grow up overnight.

Hamish's mum had made him go and talk to a woman about his 'feelings' in the end. Sometimes his mum and Jimmy came along too, though Mum had to work much longer hours now that Dad was gone. The woman had made them all agree that they had to make a decision just to carry on and not look back.

Hamish supposed there would always be hope, at least. And at least hope was something.

Anyway, now he had something to distract him.

Now he had the Pause.

'Hamish!' shouted his mum from downstairs. 'I've got so much paperwork still to do! Will you run to the shops for me?'

WH

Inside Shop Til You Pop, Hamish handed over the £5 note his mum had given him for a new tin of Mustn'tgrumbles, six eggs and a cauliflower. He collected his change, said thank you and walked straight out again, ready to jump on his bike and cycle back home.

He noticed Mr Slackjaw had repaired the beautiful blue Vespa he'd used the other day. The garage owner had been very confused about how it had ended up in such a state, but now it was spick and span and back out in front of the shop.

Hamish tied his plastic shopping bag to his handlebar and was about to set off when . . .

'**THERE HE IS**, that little *pinhead!*'

Grenville Bile was pointing right at Hamish. He was sitting on his low black bike with the really high handles.

'Stop right there, Smellerby!'

Grenville was surrounded by two fearsome new associates, sitting on their scuffed and battered old BMXs. Hamish recognised them at once. These were the rattiest, nastiest kids from St Autumnal's. Grenville had outsourced the job to another school!

One of them was Lurgie Ting. He was enormously tall. Some people said he could already get into nightclubs even though he was only eleven. He wore leather gloves, because he thought it made him look tough.

It did.

The other one Hamish recognised as Roger Flemm. This kid was ninety-eight per cent snot. He was like a snail – you could pretty much follow his trail through town. Roger's sleeves would creak and crack from all the dried nose juice he'd wipe from his nostrils every day. It was absolutely disgusting and so was he.

But what did Grenville Bile want with Hamish now?

Hamish decided he didn't want to find out. He let go of the brakes, swung the bike around and began to furiously pedal away!

But Grenville wasn't going to let him do that . . . no way! **'GETTIM!'** he yelled, and when Hamish looked behind him, he saw Grenville, thundering towards him, two fat legs pounding away on his pedals. His tubby nemesis had even pulled on his green Mexican wrestling mask, which he only ever did when he really meant business, because he thought he looked just like his favourite Mexican wrestler in this – *El Gamba*!

'Split up!' yelled Grenville to Roger and Lurgie. 'Head him off round the corner!'

Lurgie Ting went one way. Roger Flemm went the other. But Grenville stayed hot on Hamish's heels.

Hamish was panicking now. What were they going to do to him? Maybe he could get to Robin's house. But Robin would have a heart attack if he saw Hamish pedalling up with Grenville Bile right behind him. What about Jimmy? Jimmy would save him! That's what big brothers were for, wasn't it?

Wait! Felicity Gobb's street was just around the corner and Jimmy might be there!

But just as Hamish was going to turn into Aubergine Lane . . .

'GOT YA!' shouted Lurgie, springing out from nowhere and skidding to block the road.

Hamish couldn't turn – he had to keep going! Look! He could take the next right instead . . .

'STOP RIGHT THERE!' shouted Roger, skidding from round the corner, a long line of snot flinging itself out of his nose and whipping around his head.

Uuuurgh!

Hamish kept cycling straight ahead, with Grenville huffing and puffing behind him, but showing no sign of slowing.

Hamish needed a plan!

If he could just circle back to the high street and get to where there were other people, maybe Grenville would leave him alone.

So Hamish hit a right down Elderberry Avenue . . .

He looked over his shoulder, quickly . . . All three kids were gaining on him . . .

Just a little further . . . just a little further . . .

Round this corner!

Down this alley!

Over this road!

And then . . .

OOOOOOF!
BANG!
OUCH!

Hamish nearly rode straight into someone, right on the corner of the town square.

He tumbled to the ground, grazing his knees and rolling over until he went slap-bang into a fence. His bike skittered and clanked to the ground. The shopping went everywhere.

'Are you all right?'

Hamish looked up to see a girl about his age. She was wearing blue combat trousers and a blue military jumper. She had a bag over her shoulder with the letters 'PPP' written across it and a small badge stuck to one side – a badge with the St Autumnal's school sign on it. And, strangely, she had one blue streak through her otherwise jet-black hair.

'I'm fine,' said Hamish, looking around, panicked. He had nowhere to go and Grenville would be here any second. 'I'm sorry, I'm . . .'

'HA! HAHAHAHA!'

The laugh was loud and ~~malavolunt~~ evil.

Grenville had arrived. He dropped his bike to the ground. His associates did the same. The three boys each cracked their knuckles menacingly.

They had Hamish right where they wanted him. Up against a wall and just out of earshot of any nosey grown-ups, busybodies or blotter-jotters who might stop them undertaking their evil deeds.

Grenville sauntered forward, still in his El Gamba mask. Evidently, he thought he looked pretty cool in that.

Either side of him, Lurgie and Roger seemed to grow taller.

'Get up . . .' said Grenville, putting his hands on his hips. 'Get up right now—'

'Excuse me,' said the girl, interrupting. 'Why are you wearing a mask?'

'What?' said Grenville, who really didn't want to be distracted right now.

'Is it for dramatic effect?' she asked. 'Only you look like a doofus.'

Roger and Lurgie were shocked. Who was this girl? No one spoke to Grenville like this!

'I'll have you know this is a Mexican wrestling mask,' said Grenville, patiently. 'The same one worn by . . . *El Gamba*!'

He made an impressive face. The girl scrunched up her nose.

'My cousin lives in Spain,' she said. 'Doesn't "El Gamba" mean . . . the Prawn?'

'What? No!'

'Yes it does,' said the girl. '"El Gamba" means "the Prawn". What kind of name is the Prawn? The Prawn is pretty much the least frightening name of all time.'

'No it's not,' said Grenville, who felt like he was losing some of his power here. 'Shut up.'

'Oh, no, the Prawn, the Prawn!' she said, sarcastically. 'Well, I'd better do what you say, seeing as you're known as the Prawn and all. I wouldn't want to get light-to-moderate food poisoning or anything.'

Roger laughed. Lurgie pushed him to tell him to stop, then had to wipe his hand.

'Look, I'm pretty busy here,' said Grenville.

'Sorry,' said the girl. 'I must remember not to be so *shellfish*.'

Roger laughed again and even Lurgie had to admit that was a pretty good gag. *Who was this girl?* wondered Hamish.

'*Now, Ellerby*,' said Grenville, firmly. 'You need to be punished for what you did to my associates.'

'I didn't do anything to your associates,' said Hamish, who felt a little braver with this girl around. 'Honestly. They just ran at me and missed.'

'Scratch and Mole said you made them look stupid in front of everybody,' said Grenville. 'And so now I'm afraid you must pay.'

The three boys were very close to poor Hamish now. He took a deep breath, ready for whatever they had in store. Grenville suddenly took Hamish's hand, lifted it up to eye level and said . . . 'Now *that's* a nice watch.'

'It's my dad's,' said Hamish. 'Or it was. Please, Grenville, look—'

'Well, if it was your dad's, it's not like he needs it now, is it?'

Hamish started to panic. He wanted to fight them. He could feel his chest tightening with rage. This was so unfair. And they were going to take the one special thing Hamish had.

But there were three of them. And they were so much bigger than him.

'I'll just borrow it, I think,' said Grenville, pulling the watch off Hamish's wrist and tossing it casually to Roger. 'I could do with a nice new watch.'

'Leave him alone,' said the girl. 'You're a bully in a mask. The only thing you've got in common with a prawn is the size of your brain.'

Oh, don't make this worse, thought Hamish.

'I bet you've never punched anybody in your life,' she said.

'I bet you'd just hurt your knuckles if you did!'

What was this girl doing? Why was she winding Grenville up?

'Oh, yeah?' said Grenville, smiling. 'Well, Hamish, prepare to find out . . .'

And as the nasty little thug raised one chubby fist to do just that . . . and as Hamish cursed that strange girl and closed his eyes in anticipation . . .

A bright . . .

. . . brilliant . . .

FLASH!

Hamish took in the scene around him.

Grenville with his fist in the air. Roger about to wipe his nose. Lurgie with his hands on his hips. The girl with the blue streak watching it all take place.

He began to laugh, out of nothing but sheer relief!

Twice the Pause had saved him now!

Oh, thank you! Thank you!

He could do anything he wanted now. He could tweak Grenville's nose if he liked. He could kick Lurgie in the shin.

He could swap everything in Roger's pockets around so he didn't know where anything was any more. He could pull down his pants and show them his bottom if he wanted to.

Hamish had the power.

Hamish had the control.

Hamish was the greatest force in the universe!

But what Hamish wasn't banking on was this.

The most awful, horrible, blood-curdling noise . . .

A noise so awful, so horrible and so blood-curdling it is impossible to tell you exactly what it sounded like.

Except that it was awful.

And horrible.

And it could curdle your blood.

A kind of

FVAAAAAAAAAAAAAAAR!

A sort of

PHWAAEEEEEEEEEEEEER!

A type of

PHFFFVVVVAAAEEEEEER!

It was the sound of pain and fear. Of nightmares. Of hope disappearing down a screaming plughole.

The noise was everywhere, almost like it was solid. It ran through Hamish's body, making his teeth ring. It was sharp and spiked and almost too loud to handle.

He raised his hands to his ears to block it out, but it was no good. The noise was stronger than he was.

Looking around him, he saw the sky darken – how was this possible, when the world was still? This had never happened in the other Pauses. Suddenly it wasn't so great to be the only one moving around. He wanted to ask questions, to talk to the others . . . which was when he heard something else.

A roar.

The terrifying clatter of hooves.

Hundreds of hooves.

The whispers, growing louder by the second.

The hum of a huge and approaching horde!

Hamish began to feel very frightened indeed. He wanted to run. To hide. To get inside somewhere, anywhere. He wanted to be in his own room more than anything in the world. He wanted his mum. He wanted his dad.

What was coming? What was round the corner?

These were questions Hamish would quickly realise he actually did *not* want the answers to.

Because the truth was so much worse than anything he could imagine.

The Awful Truth

As they turned the corner and came into view, Hamish fell completely still.

Not because he was trying to blend in with the others.

But because what he saw made his blood run cold.

These things, these *shapes*, they were everywhere.

Starkley was overrun.

Some came on horses . . . but wait, no – not horses. These horses had *scales*. They were black as the night, black as coal and the breath that shot from their nose was black too.

Others just ran, their barbed feet clickety-clacketing on concrete and their bony fingers constantly wiggling, like skittery spiders' legs.

The awful figures wore hoods and cloaks and, when Hamish saw what was underneath, his tummy flipped and turned . . .

Pale white faces, bug eyes, two tiny pinpricks for a nose . . .

Some had monstrous tusks and smaller, round black eyes

and mouths that seemed to open half their head . . .

And the teeth! Hamish had never seen so many fearsome teeth.

He moved a fraction backwards as he realised they were coming his way – they were coming *every* way!

Stop! Hamish thought. *I can't move a muscle! I mustn't! Or else they'll grab me! Or eat me! Or do who knows what to me!*

He fixed himself in position next to Grenville and the girl. He felt the urge to chalk round his feet, but there wasn't the time!

The things came closer . . . What were they? They prodded and poked the poor people of Starkley who were stuck in the Pause. The creatures slithered about, the hum getting louder . . . They ruffled hair and slid their long, wet fingers into pockets, pulling out wallets and tissues and coins . . .

Some of them cackled as they clambered around, climbing up buildings or overturning flowerboxes . . . cracking the odd window with their sharp yellow nails as they sniffed out what was inside . . . while their scaled horses, with giant red lizard tongues, thundered noisily around.

This was chaos. Starkley was absolute chaos.

FVAAAAAAAAAAAAAR!

The noise again. Louder this time and even more painful. Hamish winced until it stopped, his eyes growing wider as he saw . . .

. . . the *tallest, most grotesquest thing he had ever seen.*

It must have been twelve feet tall with a top hat that made it taller still. Was it in charge? It was like an ogre! Or a warlock! A cross between a circus ringmaster and a witch! It made string-bean Mr Ramsface look like a toddler!

The smaller things skittered away as this giant strode into view, like fish fleeing a shark. They cowered around it. It was huge with enormous feet, the size of dogs. Wooden shoes that splintered and creaked. Knees like footballs, thighs like logs, two huge grey arms and that black top hat . . .

And there – look at that! A roll of low black fog crept into town with it, like a carpet beneath its feet . . .

Hamish totally wanted to vomit. I'm serious. This kid wanted to bend and send. He wanted to set his lunch free. He was all about fertilising the pavement.

And that was *before* the smell hit him.

This smell was the opposite of anything you've ever wanted to smell, ever. Like the weird noise, it felt to Hamish like you could touch it – that was how thick and rich and bitter it was. It was like vinegar and fish. It was like sulphur and eggs. You could almost see it as it hung in the air. It made your nose rise and your eyebrows fall. It was powerful. So powerful it could turn a white cat brown.

In its hand, the gigantic beast held some kind of crooked and shell-like bugle, which seemed to move and grow . . . Hamish almost thought it could be alive . . .

Once more it blew it –

FVAAAAAAAAAAAAAAAR!

The things became quiet.

The beast stared at them.

'BEGIN!' it suddenly roared, looking

at the town clock, while the trees began to sway from the power of his words.

Hamish found himself covered in thick raindrops of spittle that emerged from the giant thing's mouth and splatted loudly on the concrete. It was like having a shower in cabbage and pickle juice. It almost made him miss Mr Longblather.

World! Please start again! thought Hamish. Please, *world, start again!*

Next was a rising howl of joy from the things that made Hamish shake.

Stop shaking! he thought. *Don't move!*

He wanted to close his eyes, but they were welling up from the stench of that pickle juice and he was worried that if he closed his eyes a tear might fall. Then it would be Game Over.

The things were taking over Starkley, bursting through doors and slinking down sewers . . .

Hamish's eyes followed them from the edge of the square. He couldn't turn and run, because then they'd know. They'd grab him! And eat him! All he could do was watch in sheer horror as these vast things leapt from rooftops, landing on people's shoulders, getting inside their clothes, sniffing their armpits . . .

There were two of them pulling at Mr Slackjaw's jacket!

Another two were pushing a frozen Astrid Carruthers around like a ball!

Which is when Hamish noticed something . . .

The girl opposite – she was *looking* at him. She hadn't moved an inch, but her eyes were on him. She hadn't been looking at him before – how was she looking at him now?

'FIND ONE!' came the roar again, and Hamish noticed the beast had a moustache so huge it could easily have been a damp black squirrel. Its fingers were like greasy, bloated sausages, dripping fat.

What did that mean, find one? Find one *what*?

Then . . .

Sniff sniff.

Sniff sniff sniff.

Oh, no.

A *thing* was near.

It was slinking up to Hamish and his group. He could see its terrible mouth and pale, awful face, getting closer and closer.

Instinctively, Hamish glanced at the girl again. But she wasn't looking at him any more.

The thing was joined by two more, who snuffled and grunted at Hamish's feet, their tusks scraping the concrete below. Slowly, they unfolded their legs like crickets and rose up until they towered far above him.

Hamish stood in their shadow and fought the urge to whimper. He tried to control his breathing. He took a quiet breath through his nose and held it.

The things didn't seem to talk. They stalked around the kids, every once in a while lurching forward to stare into an eye or study an ear.

Ewww! Their breath smelled of old beef! It was hot and sour, as they snorted and gruntled . . .

A moment later . . . **THWACK!**

One of the things delivered a mighty slap to Grenville's thigh.

They all laughed and pointed as it wobbled.

Grenville remained perfectly still.

Another thing wanted a turn.

THWACK!

Woah! That was a really big one! They all laughed again.

EEE-EEE-EEE-EEE-EEE!

Then they all pointed at Grenville's wrestling mask and laughed at that too.

Now another one got in close to Roger's face.

It noticed the trails of snot dripping from Roger's nostrils, like a couple of bright green waterfalls.

It made a noise of appreciation.

And then, from somewhere in that dreadful head, the biggest, wartiest tongue you could ever imagine flapped its way out . . .

No! thought Hamish. *Anything but that!*

And he watched in horror as the thing slowly licked its way up that grotty boy's snotty face.

Hamish was horrified. At everything about that. He didn't want to be either of them. He could see that bristly, hairy, scratchy tongue make its way to the top of Roger's head, where it wet his hair and made the front spike up.

FVAAAAAAAAAAAAAAR!

The beast began to stomp away with its bugle in its hand and a second later the things began to bound away . . . Was it over? More of them slunk out of doorways and garages, or slid down buildings. Those closest to Hamish backed away too, pausing only to pick up a frozen cat and lick it as they left.

The sky lifted, the world brightened . . .

And there was a small, but significant . . .

'Thank goodness!' said Hamish, loudly. 'Oh, thank *goodness*!'

Grenville stared at him, his fist still in a ball.

'Well, I must say, Hamish,' he said. 'That's a very strange reaction to being told you're going to get thwunked on the nose!'

'Hahaha!' said Hamish, laughing in sheer relief. 'Hahahahaha!'

Grenville shrugged then thwunked him.

As he stood up again, still smiling, Hamish watched the boys walk away. Grenville was limping, but obviously didn't know why. He kept pointing at his thigh and shaking his head.

How long had that Pause been?

Then it hit Hamish. The Explorer. Grenville still had Hamish's Explorer.

Over their shoulders, already some way away, was the girl with the blue streak in her hair. She must have set off the moment the Pause ended, and was putting something into her bag as she walked quickly away.

Hamish looked down at where she'd been standing.

There was a chalk outline of two little feet. *Her* feet.

He *had* seen her looking at him!

Hamish suddenly knew he was not alone. The girl could move in the Pause too.

He also knew he had bigger problems than Grenville Bile. And they had tusks.

Nightfall

That night, quite understandably, Hamish was too scared to fall asleep.

The world had gone from fascinating to terrifying in the space of a Starkley afternoon.

Hamish couldn't get the things out of his mind. What were they? Why had they come?

He'd begged Jimmy to let him sleep in his room with him, but Jimmy was in a foul mood. Felicity wasn't returning his Skype requests or answering his texts, so he informed Hamish he would be 'actually concentrating on composing some pretty dark poetry this eventide?'

Robin had called round and Hamish tried to work up the courage to tell him about the evil, lolloping monsters. But then Robin screamed, because he thought he saw a burglar that turned out to be just his own reflection in the mirror. He told Hamish he'd better go home and have a lie-down after that, especially because it would be getting dark in a couple of hours.

Lastly, Hamish had tried to talk to his mum. But she was so overwhelmed by a mountain of paperwork that he lost all confidence. She kept tutting at a big red graph on her laptop and saying, 'Oh dear me, what now?'. How do you bring up the subject of enormous, slithering, white-faced monsters leaping all over town, when someone is up to their elbows in silly complaints about how much a pineapple costs, or how their windows keep cracking, or how someone thinks a dog looked at them funny?

But the really bad thing was this.

Since he'd gone to bed, Hamish had realised that it's one thing when the world stops during the day. It's easy to tell when it happens. The silence is the first thing you notice, like someone turning off a television. And it's light in the day, so you see it all: you see the car fumes that freeze from exhaust pipes. You see the way cars stop in the middle of the road as they prepare to turn left or right, their orange indicator light now no longer flashing – just on. You see people chatting outside silent cafes, not realising their conversation has paused and the thoughts they are sharing hang between them. You see the dog by the tree with his leg cocked into the air, starting what it will never know will be the longest pee of its life.

In short, there are things you can notice when the world stops during the day.

But at night?

Well, at night, it's just you.

In your room.

On your own.

In the *dark*.

Who knows what could be going on outside?

Who knows what could *be* outside?

This is what slowly began to scare Hamish as he lay there, the covers pulled up right to his nose. He held his breath and just listened, trying to hear anything that might prove the world was still going and he was safe.

But everything was quiet. He couldn't even hear his mum doing the dishes or watching the news, because she'd gone to bed ages ago.

Hamish felt very alone. Had the world Paused? Were the things coming?

And finally, in the distance, he heard the bark of a dog.

Hamish relaxed his tense shoulders, and slept, and began to dream . . .

It was a music lesson at school.

Everything had been pretty normal, until Hamish noticed one of the tubas had grown legs and started dancing. No one else seemed to think this was strange. Only Hamish could see the dancing tuba and he didn't know whether to tell anyone.

The dancing tuba (who seemed to be called Pablo) craned its neck and nodded with its fatter end at the window.

There was a blackbird there.

Hamish and the blackbird were flying high now, way up in the sky above Starkley, through cloud after cloud. Hamish was seeing the town in a way no other kid has ever seen it. The blackbird was showing him the way home.

They landed on his window ledge and Hamish clambered inside. He noticed he was in his pyjamas now. He climbed into bed and pulled the covers up tight.

And just as he was drifting off, there was a

FLASH

of light. He opened his eyes as his heart began to race and another

FLASH

lit up a silhouette at his window.

Dad? Was it his dad?

But a final slow

FLASH

showed Hamish the horrible truth.

There was a monster at his window. It just stood there, now lit by the moon, staring into his room. He could see the breath rising from its nose. He could see the tusks.

Hamish couldn't move.

He knew it had come for him.

✦

'Did you sleep well, chicken?' asked his mum, over breakfast. She was getting ready for work. Monday was going to be tough. Mind you, every day was difficult nowadays. The complaints were really flooding in. Mr Slackjaw was now more certain than ever that something was going on with his mopeds. Old Mr Neate had written his 300th furious letter about the town clock never running on time. The only thing people weren't complaining about was not having enough to complain about.

Hamish's mum was sure that it was just a matter of time though.

Hamish was still in his 'H' pyjamas. He was pretty tired. He'd stopped being scared by the dream though. He was more fascinated by Pablo the dancing tuba. If dreams were supposed to mean something, what did a shimmying Spanish brass section mean? Hamish decided that bit probably didn't mean much at all.

But, if there was one thing last night *had* taught him, it was that he didn't want to be alone. Not the next time there was a Pause - no way.

And there was only one person who could do what he could do.

He needed to find the girl with the blue streak in her hair.

Something is Amiss!

The first thing Hamish noticed as he walked into the playground that day was the noise.

An enormous group of kids were cheering and punching the air.

'Go on!' one of them shouted.

'Get stuck in!' shouted another.

'Wahey!'

Hamish could only see their backs, but he knew exactly what was happening.

There was a fight.

Fights were rather unusual at Winterbourne. The school motto was:

COME
ON
EVERYBODY,
SETTLE
DOWN

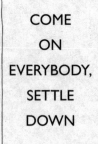

But every once in a while someone got into an argument that spilled over into something angrier. Hamish wondered who it could be and decided it was probably Grenville as usual.

But then Hamish spotted Grenville over to one side, just watching, with his mouth wide open. He was wearing The Explorer.

'YOU RINGWORM!'

Hamish frowned, turning back to the crowd. He knew that voice.

'YOU HOLD STILL, YOU OLD GOAT!'

It couldn't be . . .

'YOU LICKSPITTLE!' shouted the other person. **'GERROFF ME!'**

Hamish pushed through the crowd to get closer . . . and he had to blink once or twice to make sure what he was seeing was real.

'I WILL HAMMER YOU LIKE A PEANUT, MARGOT FUSSBUNDLER!'

yelled Mr Longblather, his face bright red and his voice quite strained.

'I WILL SIMMER YOU LIKE A SWEATY ONION, EVER LONGBLATHER!'

yelled Frau Fussbundler, who was sitting cross-legged on the ground. She had Mr Longblather in a headlock and was flicking his ear with one long finger.

'What's going on?' asked Hamish, finding Robin at the front.

'They just went crazy!' his friend replied. 'Frau Fussbundler was using Mr Longblather's favourite brown mug and he strolled right up to her and threatened to put her in detention!'

'What?'

'So she poured her coffee all over his shoes!'

'His shoes?'

'His *favourite* shoes! So he got his whistle out and blew it really close to her face! So she got her marker pen out and drew a bottom on his forehead!'

'She did *what*?'

'Then he tweaked her nose. And then she flicked his ear. And then before anyone knew what was happening they were rolling around on the floor like a couple of toddlers.'

'I'LL WRAP YOU UP LIKE A CHRISTMAS PRESENT AND POST YOU TO BELGIUM!' yelled Frau Fussbundler.

'YEAH?' replied Mr Longblather, who no one had *ever* seen be this exciting! 'WELL, I'LL STRETCH YOUR EARS UNTIL YOU CAN SAIL THERE YOURSELF!'

And, as they rolled around on the floor some more, all the kids just stared.

It was so interesting that they almost didn't notice that behind them, a small blue minivan had rolled up.

'Look,' whispered Robin, as the minivan's side door opened. 'Look who it is.'

Out of the car stepped Scratch Tuft and Mole Stunk.

They looked small and frightened and not at all like the scary kids who had threatened Hamish a few days earlier. Every scrap of fearsomeness and rebellion was gone. They looked like they were . . . *behaving*.

The two girls walked slowly into school, with their heads down and their jackets buttoned right up.

Inside the van, Hamish could see both sets of parents. So they were back. Where had they been?

'AND DON'T YOU DARE MISBEHAVE, YOU LITTLE BUGBEARS!' shouted Mole's dad, appearing through the sunroof. **'ELSE I'LL TAKE AWAY ALL YOUR TOYS AND SELL THEM TO YOUR FRIENDS!'**

All the parents in the minivan started laughing and slapping each other on the back. Their laughter was all you could hear as they drove speedily away.

Hamish and Robin exchanged a glance. Now they were certain.

Something was definitely going on with the grown-ups.

'RIGHT. I WANT PERFECT SILENCE!'

Mr Longblather held some cotton wool to his nose as he did the register. He had a bit of a nosebleed.

Already he'd given two children detention because they hadn't saluted when they entered the classroom.

'We didn't know we were supposed to salute!' they'd argued.

'Well, you know now!' said Mr Longblather. 'And you can have detention tomorrow too, for answering back!'

Their teacher seemed terribly annoyed at the world. He'd made Astrid Carruthers turn and face the back of the room, because one of her socks was slightly higher than the other. He'd made Ahmed Kahn write the phrase 'I must not sneeze in such an overly dramatic way' one hundred times in his exercise book. Johnny Fothergill had been sent to the Time Out chair just because Mr Longblather had once had his hair cut by someone whose name was *also* Johnny Fothergill and he hadn't cared for the results one bit.

Outside, Tyrus Quinn and Rex Ox were blowing confiscated footballs over the fence with the leaf blower and high-fiving.

'Can I ask you something?' Hamish whispered to Robin. 'Your cousin goes to St Autumnal's, doesn't she?'

'St Au-*bum*-nal's? Yeah,' said Robin.

'Has she ever talked about a girl with blue hair?'

'Blue hair?' said Robin.

'Well, black hair, but with one long blue bit.'

Robin shrugged.

'I can ask her later if you like.'

Robin pointed at Grenville, who was doing his usual nasal foraging.

'Isn't that your dad's watch?' he said.

Hamish nodded, sadly. How was he going to get it back? Not only was it the only thing he really had left from his dad, but he needed that watch to check how long the Pauses were getting.

'After school,' said Hamish. 'I'm going to go up to him. I'm going to steal my watch back. I'm going to . . .'

THWACK!

Where did that come from? Hamish found himself in a cloud of dust as the chalkboard eraser bounced off his bonce.

'HAMISH ELLERBY!' yelled Mr Longblather, louder than he'd ever been before. **'IT SEEMS YOU WANT DETENTION! WELL, PREPARE FOR DETENTION LIKE NEVER BEFORE!'**

Grenville turned to Hamish and smiled a sickening smile, then made a big show of checking 'his' Explorer.

Detention!

When Hamish arrived at detention, it felt weird for a lot of reasons.

It was absolutely packed, for a start. Mr Longblather must have been in an *awful* mood all day to keep this many people after school.

Every single chair, table and bit of floor space was taken. There were kids on top of filing cabinets and kids hanging off the blackboard.

It seemed like every single child in school was here. Hamish even saw some kids from *different* schools.

Only Grenville seemed to have escaped punishment. Clearly, even in the mood he was in, Mr Longblather didn't want to face the wrath of the Postmaster.

Hamish could see him now through the window. He was sitting on the wall outside the classroom in his little shorts, with a huge bag of Gambian Gobstoppers, throwing The Explorer high up into the air and catching it. Hamish felt sick. Grenville kept pretending he wasn't going to catch the watch and might simply let it drop. But probably the weirdest thing about this very, very busy detention was who was sitting at the desk next to Hamish.

It was Frau Fussbundler.

Somehow, Mr Longblather had even managed to give the *headteacher* a detention.

Frau Fussbundler seemed very ashamed, but she was also fuming and swearing revenge under her breath in German. She was far too big for the chair she was sitting in, and her knees lifted the desk right off the floor. Have you ever met Frau Fussbundler? Well, up until today, she was the last person you'd expect to find rolling around on the floor grappling with another teacher and trying to flick their ear.

Frau Margot Fuss-bundler had taught at Winterbourne forever. She was married to Dr Eric Fussbundler, the cheerful dentist who ran The Tooth Hurts on the high street. No one really knew why he was quite so cheerful. 'I'm just *filling* good!' he'd often say, because that was his little joke. He had lots of little jokes. Some of them were so little they were actually invisible.

People called him 'the King of the Dentists', because he was so good at crowns. He was particularly cheerful these days, because just last month he'd won Starkley Dental Worker of the Year.

Hamish had been to see him just a few weeks ago.

'What did you win?' Hamish had asked when he was getting his filling.

'Just a little plaque,' said Dr Fussbundler, with a toothy grin.

Hamish hadn't wanted to have that filling. I mean, who wants a filling? Really he'd only gone because his dad had made the appointment for him just a few days before he left. It sounds strange, but keeping that appointment meant something to Hamish, like by going he was making sure he stayed connected to his dad. He'd thought about the date a lot.

MAY THE 4TH, 2.30 p.m.

In a way, it had been something to look forward to. But the truth was he never really understood why his dad would book an appointment so far in advance.

'Prevention's as good as a cure, H!' his dad had said, ruffling his hair. 'Always prepare!'

The appointment itself had been a little strange too.

'Don't worry,' Dr Fussbundler had said, holding up his enormous metal machine. 'I know the *drill*!'

Robin had made fun of him for needing a filling. Robin's dental hygiene, he claimed, was second to none. Mainly because his mum made him brush his teeth for fifteen minutes before and after dinner every night.

So Hamish had laid back in the chair, quivering slightly, while Dr Fussbundler made small talk and tested his scrapers and scoopers and prodders and pokers.

'Now if I have to dash off at any point,' Dr Fussbundler had said, snapping on his blue plastic gloves, 'I'll make sure there is someone to *fill in* for me!'

BVVVRRRRR screamed the drill as he lowered it into Hamish's mouth.

'*Brace* yourself!' Dr Fussbundler had shouted.

And *BVVVVNNNNEEEEEEEEEE OOOOOOWWWW* the drill had shrieked, juddering and shuddering into Hamish's poor tooth. His whole head had started vibrating and water shot everywhere.

'A bad dentist gets on everybody's *nerves*!' Dr Fussbundler had chuckled over the cacophony. '*Nerves!* Do you get it?'

Hamish tried to nod, but now one of Dr Fussbundler's hands was all the way into his mouth. Poor Hamish watched with eyes wide as pancakes as the good doctor reached behind him for a tub of something marked **ZINOXYCLUMP™**. It was a thick grey goo like hair gel that Dr Fussbundler scooped out on a big metal spoon. He started generously slathering the stuff into Hamish's tooth.

'Going to need a lot of this!' Dr Fussbundler had yelled. 'It's going to be a hard day at the *orifice*!'

Trying to distract himself, Hamish had stared at the tub, and noticed the words **TRIAL PRODUCT – BELASKO** written on its side.

Belasko. He recognised that word from his dad's business card. It had the same logo and everything. Two black wings, one on either side of a sunflower. It must be one of the products sold by his dad's company, he thought. Well, he hoped it was a good one, seeing as it was being shovelled into his gob like this. Then he was distracted again by Dr Fussbundler clambering onto the chair and starting to fling Hamish's poor head around.

Ten minutes later, sweaty and red, Dr Fussbundler was finished.

'There – *smiles* better!' he said, mopping his brow.

'Okay, Dr Fussbundler, bye then,' Hamish said as he left, pretty bored of all the dental puns and rubbing his cheek.

Dr Fussbundler hadn't been quite as delicate as he'd hoped.

'*Tartar!*' replied Dr Fussbundler, cheerily.

'Right! **DETENTION OVER!**' shouted Mr Longblather, disturbing Hamish's thoughts about good dental hygiene. **'OUT WITH YOU!'**

Everybody ran for the door.

Unfortunately, Hamish ran straight into Grenville.

'Oh, hello, *Smellerby*,' he said, smirking. 'Would you like a sweetie?'

He'd clearly been waiting for Hamish just to do this. He held out a large paper bag with Madame Cous Cous's face on the front.

Hamish frowned. Was this a trick?

'Oh, hang on, I forgot!' said Grenville, with enormous smugness. 'You're not allowed any, are you? No, I saw your name on the list in the sweet shop. Banned for life, it said. You and *all* your friends!'

Hamish stared at Grenville's bag. It was topped to the brim with Madagascan Mouth Melters and at least four of those brand-new Turkish Twizzlers. His mouth began to water.

'I'm going to the wrestling at the town hall a bit later,' Grenville said. 'My mum "found" some spare tickets.'

Oh, I bet she did, thought Hamish.

'Do you have the time, by the way? I don't want to be late!'

Grenville knew full well Hamish didn't have the time.

'Oh, actually, it's okay,' he said, checking The Explorer on one chubby wrist. 'I'll just check my watch.'

And as he waddled away, dropping sweet wrappers behind him and belching, Hamish could not *wait* for the next Pause.

He knew *exactly* what he was going to do – monsters or not.

14

Let's Make a Plan!

In his bedroom that night, Hamish worked out a plan.

There were two parts to 'Plan 1'. He called them 'A' and '2'.

A) Find the girl with the blue streak in her hair and find out what the heck was going on with those awful lolloping monster things.

2) Get Grenville back!

Let's say the next Pause was – ooh, I dunno – thirteen minutes and thirteen seconds long.

If it happened during schooltime, Hamish knew one thing: the girl with the blue streak would also be at *her* school. All he'd have to do is hop on one of Mr Slackjaw's scooters and whizz round to St Autumnal's sharpish to find her. That was A sorted.

If the Pause happened out of school, well . . . the girl could be anywhere. So Hamish reckoned he'd be better off using the time to go round to Grenville's house and teach that little oik a lesson. That was when *1* would come into action.

Excellent, thought Hamish, as he put his favourite blue and white 'H' pyjamas on. *It's always best to have a plan. And another plan too.*

He looked down at his updated PSK on the bed.

After the last Pause, he'd added a few new items to the kit, including a miniature bottle of travel deodorant he'd found under Jimmy's bed. He was pretty sure those monsters could smell children's fear, so a hearty spray of 'New Tropical Pumpkin Man-Mist' might well help him avoid their noses. Although it *would* mean he would stink pretty badly of pumpkins.

Hamish moved to his window and watered the sunflower that sat in front of it, in its little blue pot.

The sky was growing dark outside. It was getting late.

Through the window of the house next door, he could see Mr Ramsface with his ukulele, playing the two little Ramsfaces a goodnight song. Mrs Ramsface was leaning on the door frame to one side, gazing at them all adoringly.

Hamish wanted to look away, but couldn't stop staring at the cosy scene. He wished things could go back to how they were. When Dad was here to read him stories, and

Mum wasn't too busy to lean on *his* door frame, and when Jimmy wasn't quite so fifteen. He leaned his head against the window, and let his eyes grow heavy to the sound of the *tick-tick-tick-tick-tick* of his bedside alarm clock.

He went over the plans again in his head.

A) If it happens tomorrow at school, I'll find the girl.

2) If it happens tomorrow at home, I'll go and get my watch back and make Grenville pay.

What Hamish couldn't have known is that the next Pause would happen a lot sooner than that.

15

The Wee Small Hours

Sometime in the wee small hours, Hamish woke.

He opened his eyes and saw the blue light of the moon stretching across his ceiling and down into his room. Maybe he could get straight back to sleep if he was lucky.

But as he closed his eyes, and wiped the drool from his cheek, he felt a little unsettled.

You know in films where they say something like: 'It's quiet – *too* quiet'?

Well, that's how it felt. Too quiet.

Hang on. Where was the *tick-tick-tick-tick-tick* of his alarm clock?

Hamish's blood ran cold.

He sat up. He listened. He listened hard. But there was no ticking clock.

Slowly, quietly, he turned the clock to face him.

It had *stopped*.

Hamish gulped hard and lay back down. He squeezed his

eyes shut and pretended to be asleep. He wanted to shout out, but if the world had stopped then everyone would be frozen.

Maybe it's the batteries, he thought, trying to reassure himself. *Maybe they just ran out and that's why the clock stopped.*

But Hamish had to be sure. He needed to be certain.

Somehow he found the strength to pull his covers back and slide out of bed. As silently as he could, he crept towards the window. The world was perfectly still, but it was always still at night, wasn't it? Wait, look over there . . .

A blackbird hung suspended about a metre from his window, its wings out, and silhouetted against the moon. Leaves from trees were frozen in the air around it. It looked like it was about to hit the glass – like Hamish could reach out and touch it.

Again? thought Hamish.

He slid the sunflower on his windowsill to one side so he could reach the lock.

Which is when a noise caught him off guard.

Not the noise of a weird bugle this time, but something that made him even more fearful and queasy. It was a noise like a thousand whispers and it was getting louder, and louder and louder. Hamish backed away from the window . . . his eyes were wide and his shoulders were stiff.

Not those things again . . . not those terrible things.

Where were they coming from? What did they want? Were they coming to get him? And then what? Eat him?

He wanted to turn around and run for his bed . . . he wanted to scream . . . he wanted to spray the place in Tropical Pumpkin deodorant! But, as he stepped backwards he noticed the blackbird again. It would hit his window the second the world started again and he couldn't let that happen. So, quickly, he strode back to his window, opened it, turned the bird around, closed his window and –

THERE THEY WERE!

The things, the awful, white-faced, black-cloaked things . . . Tusks and whispers and clickety-clacketing feet . . .

The coal-black, red-tongued lizard horses . . .

The horde poured round the side of the Ramsfaces' house like a gas, filling up the garden, their hiss growing by the second.

Hamish remained rooted to the spot. He couldn't move now. He had to stay still, just as he'd done the other day in town. Just as the girl with the blue streak in her hair had done too.

He watched in horror as six of the things started to scamper up the Ramsfaces' drainpipe, and with their long nails began to trace around the outside of the children's window, slicing around it to open it.

Three or four others were doing the same to the back door, while even more of them prowled around the garden, keeping an eye out.

What did they want with the Ramsfaces?

Suddenly the back door burst open and two things lurched out, carrying what looked to be some kind of ragdoll in their arms.

Hamish tried not to scream as he realised – it was Mr Ramsface! The man was still in his bright pink pyjamas as he was passed down the line, roughly thrown from thing to thing. The door slammed shut behind them as they poured out of the house, taking poor Mr Ramsface with them.

Hamish wanted to bang on the window and shout at them to stop, but he couldn't even move. His heart was thumping in his ears and the hair was standing up on the back of his neck, and then he felt colder than he had ever done . . .

. . . *as he made eye contact with a thing down below.*

This one wasn't backing away like all the others.

It was standing directly below Hamish's house, in his

garden, staring up at the window.

It cocked its head, trying to work out why a boy would be staring out of his window at this time of the morning. What was this boy doing there when the world stopped?

Slowly, the thing broke away from the rest of the group and headed towards Hamish's house.

It was coming.

Hamish could hear it testing his drainpipe, pulling at it, clanking it against the wall.

Oh, no, he thought. *What do I do? What do I DO?*

Hamish could hear the thing as it hoisted itself up, pulling itself up the drainpipe, its nails catching the window frame below, grunting and slathering as it made its way up the side of the house . . .

Stay still, thought Hamish. *Stay completely still, and—*

But now here it was.

Enormous. Taking up almost the whole of the window frame. Blocking out the moon.

Its bony fingers were scraping the window as it tried to find purchase.

Its breath was fogging the glass as Hamish tried not to show he was breathing. The thing saw the blackbird, suspended by the window, and screeched as it swiped it away with a heavy wet fist. The poor bird spun and flipped as it shot through the air then dropped like a stone into a hedge below.

Now the thing stared at Hamish. It looked him up and down, with black eyes that seemed almost to glow – and as it dropped its gaze, it noticed the sunflower that sat between them and flinched away from it slightly.

Tusks tapped the glass and Hamish could hear its neck creaking as it lowered its head, like it was made out of old wet leather. They were eye to eye now, with the thing staring so hard at Hamish that it felt like it was trying to read his thoughts.

It knows I'm faking! thought Hamish, as the thing's eyes bulged once and once only as it realised . . .

. . . *that Hamish wasn't frozen!*

And, just as Hamish was about to scream and make a run for his mum's room—

FVVVVAAAAAAAAAAARRRRRRR!

The thing's eyes bulged wider now, but this time in panic. It looked at the sunflower and then at Hamish once more.

FVVVVAAAARRRRRRR!

It reached for the drainpipe and started to slide down, not taking its awful black eyes off Hamish as it did so.

Hamish remained still, but let his eyes drop slightly so he could watch the thing bounding over the bins outside the Ramsfaces' house and bend a tree almost backwards as it leapt away and into the night. . .

FLASH

The world started again.

The blackbird rustled in the bushes below, then flapped away, stunned.

But Hamish didn't feel much relief.

They know about me, he thought, with a growing sense of panic, sitting back down on the bed. *Now they know about me.*

16

The Morning After
the Night Before

If there was one thing Hamish could be certain of, it was this: the time to act was now!

The trouble was he didn't really know *what* action he should take.

How is a ten-year-old boy supposed to ward off a horde of marauding monsters plundering through Britain's Fourth Most Boring Town?

Having spent the night thinking about it, Hamish was beginning to feel his PSK might be a little lacking. There's only so much he could do with a Chomp and a small whistle and he suddenly felt vastly unprepared for what now seemed like it could be an apocalypse of some sort.

He'd had an idea, though. It was of the most minuscule variety, but it was still an idea. The thing had acted very weirdly last night when it spotted the sunflower on his windowsill. It had definitely flinched. Were they allergic? Or did it just not know what one was? Whatever the reason,

Hamish decided some sunflower seeds might come in handy. He'd plant them in the garden. Maybe he'd plant them all over Starkley. So he found an old matchbox in his dad's desk marked **BELASKO**, poured out some of the matches and added a handful of Farmer Jarmer Sunflower Seeds from the back of his mum's baking cupboard. He shoved the matchbox in his back pocket and immediately felt better. Between that and his PSK at least he had some things covered.

But there had to be more he could do.

Maybe he could alert the media. Then he remembered the *Starkley Post* only came out on Mondays. He'd have to wait *days* for the story to break!

What if he told the army then? But what general in their right mind would believe a story like this? He'd be lucky if they sent a couple of Scouts and a Brownie to secure the area.

What's more, the Pauses seem to be happening with greater and greater frequency. And Hamish had no idea what the pattern was.

There had been Saturday in town, for example. And then when he went to get eggs. And then there was last night. Were the Pauses picking up speed, as well as lasting longer?

144

His dad always said that every good adventurer needed a guardian. Someone to look over them. He would tell Hamish, over Boggle and hot chocolate, that a good guardian was like a good shepherd. 'And every sheep needs a shepherd, Hamish,' he'd said.

Well, his dad wasn't here any more. And Hamish didn't have a guardian or a shepherd or anything like that. Unless he plucked up the courage to tell Jimmy? He was always playing video games with zombies and evil bat monsters and stuff. Maybe some of that training had paid off.

But Jimmy – sorry, *James* – was in a bad mood that morning, because Felicity Gobb still wasn't returning his calls. Hamish had seen over his shoulder at the table that he'd been working on a brand-new poem to try and win her over, entitled simply 'Felicity'.

OH, FELICITY, FELICITY
YOUR NAME'S LIKE ELECTRICITY
I MUSTN'T BE PERNICKETY
BUT MARRY ME, FELICITY!!!

Underneath 'Felicity', Jimmy had scribbled out the words 'toxicity', 'Sicily', 'polygamy' and 'growth industry', as he'd had trouble making them rhyme. Nevertheless, Hamish felt that Jimmy's poetic instincts had been spot on. Felicity was a much nicer name to rhyme with than Gobb.

FELICITY GOBB
EATS CORN ON THE COB

And that was as good as it got.

Now, if there are any grown-ups reading this (and there better not be), it's very important you understand: kids sometimes need to skip school. Only occasionally, but sometimes there are vital things that need to be done and they're not going to do themselves. Hamish had never skipped school in his life. He had a feeling it might be illegal. That said, he also knew that desperate times call for desperate measures.

'So, yeah, bye, Mum,' he said at the door, nervously. 'I'm just off to school. School is where I'm going. I'm definitely going to school now.'

'Er, okay,' said his mum, distracted as usual. She was clearing the breakfast plates away, trying to find her phone and fix her hair and get her bag ready for work, all at the same time. 'Have a nice day, chicken.'

'I will, Mum,' he said, blushing. 'And you have a nice day too.'

'Nice day? I wish!' she said. ' Complaints are through the roof!'

She pointed at the laptop on the kitchen table. The big red graph she was always looking at showed a long, rising line with little sad faces all along it.

'I don't know what's happening this year, but that graph is the *bane* of my life, Hamish!' she said, shaking her head. 'The town clock seems *unfixable* and Mr Slackjaw's lost *yet another* moped!'

She picked up the television remote and held it to her ear, thinking it was her phone.

'Great!' she said, annoyed. 'And now my phone's out of battery!'

Hamish saw his moment, and started to creep away, making an innocent face.

'Oh, and Hamish . . .'

Curses! Had she seen through his lie about going to school?

But whatever it was his mum was about to say, she stopped right there. Because over Hamish's shoulder, she had spotted something.

There was a police car outside the Ramsface residence.

Mrs Ramsface was leaning on the door frame, dabbing her eye with a hankerchief while the policeman had his hands on his hips and was shaking his head, puzzled.

'Oh . . .' said Hamish's mum.

Hamish had a strong urge to run up to the policeman and tell him that Mr Ramsface had been taken in the night by some monsters with a sort of lizard horse.

And then he realised how that might sound.

He needed more information first. And he knew where he might get it.

It was time for Plan 1: Part A.

17

The Girl with the Blue Streak in Her Hair

Hamish was determined that this would work.

And why should he wait for a Pause before finding the girl with the streak in her hair? It's not like she only existed in the Pause. The rest of the time she'd be walking around Starkley, doing precisely the kinds of things that Hamish was doing.

Eating. Sniffing. Scratching. The lot.

She was about his age, after all. And that meant that, right now, she'd probably be on her way to school, carrying that bag of hers with the St Autumnal's badge.

Hamish didn't like St Autumnal's. He thought it had ideas above its station. They played hockey and cricket instead of footie. Some of them learned tennis in the summer. At least twelve of the kids carried briefcases. And their motto – oh, dear – was in *Latin*.

It had been the headteacher's, Allegory Principle's, idea. He thought it would inspire and unite the children and teachers. It was supposed to remind them to seize the day and make every moment in life count. It was supposed to celebrate all the opportunities that life throws our way. It was:

MEMENTO MORI

Which means: REMEMBER – YOU **WILL** DIE.

It has to be said, there are more inspiring mottos.

Hamish stood outside St Autumnal's enormous black school gates, waiting to see if he could spot the girl. He felt very self-conscious in his slightly scruffy Winterbourne uniform, loitering by some bins.

First he saw Lurgie Ting lolloping into school, cowering from his father, who seemed rather upset about something.

Then Roger Flemm trundled by, wiping his nose and flicking the snot at a bench, the way Spider-Man shoots webs from his wrist.

Then came tiny Ratchett Gobb with his huge eyes and his little red lunchbox. That was weird. Felicity usually walked with him to school.

But no sign of a girl with a blue streak in her hair.

Hamish waited until the big gold bell at the top of

the school began to ring.

He started to feel uneasy.

What if the things had got the girl?

Did that mean he might be next?

Hamish decided to run back to school. He could say he was late, because he had a dentist's appointment. I mean, that was sort of true. He *had* had one. It's just that it was ages ago. And, if they asked him to provide them with a note, he could just sing them a musical note and hope that that was charming and funny enough to let him get away with it.

But no.

Think of the trouble he'd get into, the way the teachers had been acting lately.

Instead, he resigned himself to having to spend the day hiding in the park. As he turned a corner towards it, he spotted something a little unusual some way up the street.

Someone was in a rubbish skip.

They were flinging old bits of wood and plastic over their shoulder. They had a school tie around their head and their sleeves rolled up.

And even from this distance Hamish could just make out a streak of blue.

When she heard someone approaching, the girl stood to attention, like a meerkat in the Kalahari Desert.

'Oh, you again,' she said, as if everything was perfectly normal, and the last time the two of them met hadn't been when they were surrounded by those dreadful things.

'What are you doing in a skip?' asked Hamish, because it seemed like that was a good question to start with.

'Scavenging,' she replied, without looking at him. 'I suggest you do the same. We have to use all the time we have, seeing as the Pauses are getting longer.'

So he was right. She hadn't been frozen like everyone else.

'You call them Pauses as well?' he said, quietly, in case

anyone overheard and thought they were mad.

'Well, what else would you call . . . a pause?' she said, simply. 'Pause seems to be the best word to describe a pause. And anyway, I'm just getting what I need.'

She picked up a large camping backpack and swung it onto her back. It was almost three times the size of her.

'What's in there?' asked Hamish.

'Supplies.'

'I've got supplies too!' he said, remembering his PSK. 'What's in yours?'

'Batteries. Kitchen roll. Toothpaste. First aid kit.'

Oh, thought Hamish. *That's a bit better than a couple of Chomps and a whistle.*

'*Spare* batteries. *Spare* kitchen roll. *Spare* toothpaste. *Spare* first aid kit,' she continued.

'Right, I see, and—'

'Freezable food. *Non*-freezable food. Water. *Powdered* water.'

'*Powdered* water?'

'Yes. You just add water to the powder, and it turns into water. And, apart from all that, I've got everything you need to survive life during the Pause. Scissors, magnifying glass, fake moustache, the lot.'

'What's your name?' asked Hamish.

The girl looked dubious.

'Why do you want to know?' she said, casting her eyes around suspiciously. 'What if you're one of Them?'

'One of who?'

'You know very well who,' she said, before adding, quite dramatically, 'one of . . . the Terribles.'

Terribles? Is that what the things Hamish had been seeing were called? And how could she think he was one of *them*? They were horrible with tusks and slime and stink. Hamish looked nothing like one of them! Not even when he *really* needed a bath!

'Do you mean—'

'I mean the *Terribles*,' said the girl. 'You saw them. I know you did. Those ginormous awfuls. Those monstrous ghastlies. You better make sure they don't know you're a Pausewalker.'

A Pausewalker, thought Hamish. *I'm a Pausewalker.*

'The last thing the Terribles need to know is that there are Pausewalkers in Starkley. Do you have any idea what they'd do to you if they knew you were just pretending to be Paused?'

Hamish thought about the night before and shivered. Had

that creature at his window worked it out? He decided not to tell the girl.

'I'm Hamish,' he said. 'Hamish Ellerby. I go to Winterbourne.'

He held his hand out for her to shake, but she just looked at it and shook her head.

'I *know* you do.'

Hamish was amazed.

'*How*?' he asked.

'Well, you're wearing a Winterbourne uniform, for a start,' she said.

Oh. Right. Hamish lowered his head.

The girl stared him up and down, then hoisted herself out of the skip.

'So how much do you know about the Terribles?' she asked, landing expertly on the pavement.

Hamish shrugged.

And so the girl with the blue streak in her hair began to tell him all about the world of the Terribles.

Which means I suppose I should tell you too.

Have you ever found a bruise and not known how you got it?

Could have been a Terrible.

Have you ever lost a sock and not known how you lost it? Or found a toy where you definitely didn't leave it? Or closed a window, but found it open?

Terribles, Terribles, terrible Terribles.

Here is what I know for a fact. They work by something they call the pecking order. There are the lows, the mids and the others.

Low Terrible

The lows are the most common Terribles. They're the bruisers. They can't help themselves. They might thumble or slurch past you while you're stuck still in the Pause, clickety-clacking their nails on the floor as they do so, and then for no reason whatsoever – *thwack!* – they'll deal you a punch. Or a flick. Or a pinch. The really nasty ones will scratch. No one likes those ones. Oh, and they stink! Have you ever smelled a really horrible smell and everyone blamed you for it? Well, that was probably them.

Unless it really *was* you, of course.

Then, higher up in the pecking order, are the mids. These

ones are all bug eyes
and pincers and horribly
slickety-wet to the
touch.

Yeuch!

They're more interested
in money than anything
else. The mids steal,
pilfer, nab and nick.
Can't find your wallet?
Guess who. Money box

Mid Terrible

mysteriously a little lighter this morning? I wonder why.
Hole in your trouser pocket where you're sure you put that
£2 coin your Uncle Xavier gave you?

Well, they probably burnt a hole in your pocket, didn't
they?

And then . . . right at the top of the pecking order, there
are the WorldStoppers themselves. So evil only long words
will do. Malicious. Murderous. Malodorous. And yes –
malevolent!

They are too terrible to look at for long and too awful to
even think about.

But we must!

The WorldStoppers lick at their long, thick, waxy moustaches. Moustaches that are stiff and solid and curled at the end like a mammoth's tusks!

And not just on the men!

They carry whips in fat, meaty, greasy hands that are freezing cold to the touch. And they have big bottoms, as ripe and plump as old brown pears.

Thwack-ash! goes the sound of the whip.

The WorldStoppers badger and bully and belittle the Terribles. They try and dress a little like humans. Goodness only knows why, because they wouldn't fool a chipmunk. They are huge and loud and awful and smart and they won't leave Starkley alone.

Not *ever*.

Oh, and of course they hate children. Especially ones like you. But, so far, they've left kids alone. Adults are much easier pickings.

Unless, of course, they think you are a child who knows about them.

Because they have to keep their secret.

Hang on – *you* know about them now, don't you?

Oh, dear.

Hamish and the girl stood and stared at each other. They were nearly at the corner of the road now. The girl adjusted her huge backpack as she decided which way to walk.

'I'll give you a tip, Hamish,' she said. 'The clock on the town hall is the only one in Starkley that tells the real time. People think it runs fast, but that's only because it keeps going even during the Pause. So, when the Pause is over, everyone thinks it's wrong. But it's the only one that's right.'

'My mum would be delighted if she knew that.'

'Why?'

'She works in the Complaints Office,' said Hamish. 'Everyone's always complaining about the clock. She's got this graph she's obsessed with that shows all the angry letters and phone calls she gets!'

The girl crossed her arms.

'Well, it's actually the only clock that works.'

Hamish half-smiled.

'Erm,' he said. 'Not . . . the only one.'

She wrinkled up her nose.

'What do you mean?'

'My dad's watch,' he explained. 'It's called The Explorer and it's not stopped in any of the Pauses.'

'What?' said the girl. 'Are you serious? Where is it? We

need that!' She smiled for the first time Hamish had seen.

And then she stopped smiling, as she realised something.

'You mean the watch that the big prawn bully took from you . . .' she said, and Hamish nodded. 'Well, you need to get that back. You have no idea how useful that will be when the Terribles return.'

Hamish shivered.

'Look,' she said. 'You never know when they'll be back. Sometimes a Pause is just a Pause. And sometimes a Pause . . . is *terrible*.'

'But . . . but . . .' started Hamish, still completely and utterly shocked by what she'd told him.

'Yes?' said the girl, looking bored again.

'But what do they *want*?' he said. 'What do the Terribles *want*?'

The girl put her hands on her hips.

'They want the grown-ups,' she said, fixing him with a stare that sent shivers down his spine. 'They want the grown-ups, and then they'll want *us*.'

They Want What?

Hamish and the girl-with-the-blue-streak-in-her-hair-whose-name-he-still-did-not-know sat on the bench by the town clock and rested their feet on her huge backpack.

Around them, the people of Starkley went innocently about their business. Two dogs started to bark at each other. A man dropped a coin and shouted a rude word. Mr Slackjaw stood outside Slackjaw's Motors, staring at his last few Vespas and shaking his head. There was a policeman next to him taking notes. And, to their side, a lady began to hammer a poster into a tree that read:

COME TO THE FAIR!

'Don't you ever feel you should tell someone?' said Hamish, pointing at the people milling around. 'Is it just us that know?'

The girl nodded and took a lick of a lollipop.

'Yes. It's just us. No one else knows. Just you and me. Now look at this . . .'

She unfolded a piece of paper. It had a chart on it, and various workings-out in bright blue and red pen. It had the name 'Elliot' at the bottom.

'Who's Elliot?' asked Hamish.

'Never mind,' she said, dismissively. 'By my calculations, based on the length and frequency of recent Pauses, we can expect another one at around ten to six this evening.'

'So they're coming?' said Hamish, glancing nervously around. 'They're coming again?'

'The Terribles don't use every Pause for their evil,' she said. 'Sometimes they don't show up at all. I think some of the Pauses must be used for resting, or admin.'

'Admin?' said Hamish.

'You don't take over the world without at least a little planning,' she replied, knowingly.

'Aren't you terrified?' asked Hamish. 'How can you be so calm?'

'I used to be scared,' she said. 'But not any more. I'm not scared of *anything* any more.'

'Last night they took my neighbour,' said Hamish. 'I didn't know they *took* people. What do they want with the grown-ups? And how do you know so much about all this?'

The girl's face softened a little.

'I know, because they took my parents,' she said, quietly.

A thought began to form at the back of Hamish's mind. His heart swelled a little and something flipped in his tummy.

'What do you mean they took your parents?' he asked.

'I mean,' said the girl, her stare turning to a look of sadness, 'that one day my parents were there, in the house with me, and then one day they weren't.'

'So you just woke up and—'

'And they were gone.'

Hamish didn't quite know what to say. He wanted to tell her about his own dad and the day the Vauxhall hadn't returned, but it felt too selfish somehow. This was *her* moment.

'I looked for them,' she said. 'I thought maybe I'd forgotten they were going to visit my auntie or something. But then I saw they'd left their phones at home and the car was still there. So I waited and waited. I stayed at home all day. And, as it got darker and darker, I got more and more frightened. When it got to around one in the morning, I'd just decided to call the police when—'

'The sky flashed?'

'Yes,' she said.

'And the Terribles came out?'

'Oh, Hamish,' she said. 'It was the worst. They arrived on their Requines.'

'Requines?'

'Haven't you seen them? The Requines are the horrible lizard-horse things the Terribles ride about on.'

Hamish shuddered as he recalled the horrible creatures.

'They were slinking around my street. The whole world was still. They were creeping into houses and they stole old Mr Neate who lived next door. They just flung him over their shoulders like he was a bag of old nuts,' she said.

'So what did you do?'

'I did nothing! I just kept still like everyone else. And they didn't seem to notice me, so . . . I've been doing it ever since.'

Hamish could see this girl was a fighter, living on her own with no one to tell about what had happened to her parents.

'I ran out of money quickly so I used to just go to Lord of the Fries every night and take fishburgers,' she said. 'My fridge was packed with them. But then I realised I could use the Pause to do shopping and now I'm pleased to say I've discovered the benefits of vitamins and five-a-days.'

She made a pompous face.

'But why haven't you told anyone?' he asked.

'In case the Terribles find out it was me who told!' she said. 'I thought I was the only person in the world who knew. It always used to happen at night so I could hide away. And anyway . . . I thought that if I watched and observed for long enough then maybe I could find my parents again.'

She looked at him very seriously.

'Because here's the thing, Hamish,' she said. 'I think they're taking a lot of grown-ups, but it's the weak ones that return to Starkley. They're the ones that are easy to brainwash and come back . . . *processed*. Like bad cheese. All curdled and stinky. I'm sure the strong adults, like my parents, are out there somewhere. They won't give in. The Terribles have *got* them. But the weak ones come back processed and mean.'

Hamish thought about it.

Mr Longblather was certainly meaner than usual.

Frau Fussbundler too.

What about Tyrus Quinn? Rex Ox, with his football-firing leaf blower?

And – my goodness, *yes*! – Madame Cous Cous and her awful big stick!

The girl was right. It was perfectly clear that adults *were* getting meaner, so maybe the Terribles were processing them and sending them back!

'The day after he was taken,' said the girl, 'old Mr Neate returned. He kicked his cat then put up a sign on his lawn saying Junk Mailers Will Be Shot! Now he just sits outside his house, throwing apples at children and making rude hand gestures at the vicar.'

Hamish was having trouble making sense of it all.

'But *why* are the Terribles turning people mean?' he asked.

'So that we fight. So that we argue. So that the world is a horrible place that we don't even want any more. I think they've started in Starkley, because it's so boring that hardly anyone ever comes here. They're testing things out and, if it works, I think they'll turn the *whole world* mean. And that's when they'll take over. When we're too mean to care.'

Hamish was horrified. Could the very future of life on earth be at stake – right here in Starkley?

If so, it looked like it might have to give its Fourth Most Boring Town certificate back.

Hamish had one more question. He was almost too scared to ask, but he knew he had to.

'My dad didn't come home one night,' he said, carefully, avoiding her eye. 'Do you think he might have been…taken?'

The girl smiled a gentle smile.

'I don't know, Hamish,' she said. 'It's possible. But I just don't know. Was he weak or strong?'

He was the strongest, thought Hamish. *He was the tallest! And he'd never give in to a bunch of ugly monsters!*

But at the same time . . . what if he *hadn't* been taken? What if one day he'd just woken up and he was just bored of his life?

Bored of Hamish?

Maybe it was better never to know, because if that was the truth, it was almost worse than any bunch of rampaging monsters.

'I have to go,' said the girl, pointing up at the clock. 'I've got a meeting.'

'A meeting? A meeting with who?'

'Never you mind with who,' she said. 'And anyway, it's *whom*.'

She heaved her huge backpack onto her little shoulders.

'When will I see you again?' he said. 'Or is it *you*?'

She smiled, but said nothing.

'Later on?' he tried. 'During the next Pause?'

'You know what you need to do during the next Pause,' she said, turning back to face him. 'You need to get your watch back. Something like that could really help us in the fight.'

Us? thought Hamish.

'And one more thing,' she said. 'You said your mum works in the Complaints Office. You said she had a graph. One that showed all the complaints.'

Hamish nodded, confused.

'Bring it next time. Okay?'

'Um . . . okay?' he replied.

'Maybe we were meant to meet, Hamish Ellerby,' she said, as she began to walk away.

'Wait – what's your name?' he said. 'Please?'

'Alice,' said the girl, without turning around. 'My name is Alice Shepherd.'

Grevenge!

Several hours later, Hamish crouched outside number nine Knotweed Lane with a determined look on his face and a piece of paper in his hand.

On the paper were the words:

Plan 1, Part 2(b): Get that watch.

He was hiding in a bush outside Grenville's house and had been hiding there since half past five.

It was starting to get rather uncomfortable.

He hoped that Alice Shepherd had been right and that the next Pause was coming, and soon because – honestly – his bottom was so numb you could use it for bongos and he'd never notice.

While he waited, Hamish looked up at the house.

Even though it was the same as all the other houses on the street, the Biles had somehow managed to make theirs look rather more fearsome. Apart from the single, spiky bush that Hamish was currently crouched inside, the garden had been concreted over and there was a jagged metal fence at around kid-height. The roof tiles were wonky and covered in black moss. The sun never seemed to shine on this house.

Tubitha 'Postmaster' Bile had put up thick, dusty black curtains in every room and she never, ever opened them. Grenville said it was so they could protect their many treasures. He didn't want any old person peeking through his windows and checking out his Super Action Rascals. And the black curtains stopped harmful UV rays from fading his priceless collection of original movie posters too, which was handy.

FLASH!

Alice had been *right*.

Cautiously, Hamish tiptoed from the bush and tapped the doorknob gently.

He'd heard that the Postmaster had wired up all the electricity in the house so that if someone turned up unexpectedly and tried the handle, they'd get a nasty shock and their hair would catch fire. It seemed safe enough today. So he tried turning it.

He was in!

Grenville's hallway was packed with dozens of old, faded oil paintings of Biles from history.

There was Lord Heronimus Bile, with a huge great beard the size of a stoat.

Oh, hang on, no – that *was* a stoat! A stoat the size of a beard!

Heronimus Bile and his 'associates' had been the terror of olde London, training stoats to pretend to be beards so they could pickpocket people's top pockets.

And there was Dame Violet Bile, inventor of Wartaway Wart Juice. She'd claimed her wart juice warded away warts, when actually all it did was herd them all together to form one big giant wart.

There was Billy Bile, the Billericay Bicycle Burglar. There was Bernie Bile, the Big Badger Baiter of Bow. And there was Bunty Bile, the part-time estate agent from just outside Stockport.

Men, women, short, tall, long hair, short hair, bearded or with stoats – it didn't matter – they all seemed to have the exact same mean face as Grenville.

Hamish shuddered and looked around. There was a green door at the top of the stairs with loads of grubby handprints all over it and a big sign that said:

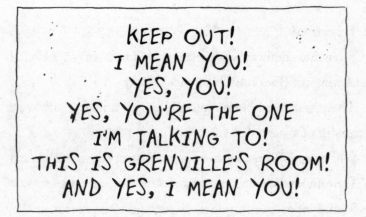

KEEP OUT!
I MEAN YOU!
YES, YOU!
YES, YOU'RE THE ONE
I'M TALKING TO!
THIS IS GRENVILLE'S ROOM!
AND YES, I MEAN YOU!

For a second, Hamish was stung by a tiny iota of jealousy. How come Grenville had it all? All those toys to have all that fun with. How come he deserved cool things and Hamish didn't?

He pushed open the door to what he was sure would be an Aladdin's cave of wondrousness, only to be rather surprised.

Grey walls.

Grey floor.

A grey ceiling.

A plain bed with one lumpy pillow and a rather limp grey duvet.

And *no* toys.

No complete set of Super Action Rascals. No big-screen TV. No computer. No books, no chairs, no posters, no colour and no *fun*.

There was a dirty-looking desk that just had one book called *The World's Funniest Tractors* lying open and a half-filled jam jar marked 'Fruits of My Nose'. Grenville's prized El Gamba wrestling mask was hung up rather proudly on a bent brass nail in the wall.

Where was all the stuff he was always banging on about? The stuff he always said made him better and cooler than everyone else?

Wait – do you smell that?

There was the worst, most awful smell in the air.

It was putrid. It was gaseous. It was stomach-churning. And it was just hanging there, frozen in time. It was almost wet in the air, like it was coating Hamish's face with a thin gel of awful. Imagine how an aeroplane leaves a vapour trail in the sky long after it's flown by. Well, it turns out that's how a smell was when it became trapped in the Pause. Hamish found he was able to actually step in and out of it (and he preferred stepping out of it).

Hamish didn't want to follow that stink, but bitter experience told him he'd find Grenville at the end of it.

Down the dark and rancid hallway he walked, peanut shells cracking underfoot like they were bones in a forest, until he came to another door.

He pushed it open, but realised immediately that this wasn't the one he was looking for.

Inside the dimly-lit room, under a brown chandelier, between a brown set of walls, and on a bright green carpet, was the Postmaster herself.

She sat at a dark wooden table and looked as if she had probably been mid-grunt when the Pause struck. She was so close that Hamish could see the tufts of black, wiry hair sprouting from the moles on her arms, like spiders hatching from a bumpy, thick egg. Six or seven flies hung still in the air around her, stuck in the smoke from her nasty fat cigar. She had a bowl of peanuts and a spoon. And she was surrounded – absolutely surrounded – by brightly-coloured parcels.

Christmas presents, birthday presents, wedding presents. All of them piled up high. They were stacked up on top of one another, crammed into cubbyholes and spread out all over the floor like a present-puddle.

Hamish could see some of the labels . . .

TO ASTRID, LOVE GRANNY

TO ROBIN, FROM WEE UNCLE TONY

So many of them! This must be every present that had been 'lost in the post' for months.

Oh, the Biles were awful!

Above the Postmaster's head was some kind of giant map of Starkley. It had dozens of thick red arrows pointing up and down and left and right, from the old grey bridge in the woods right the way to the clock in the middle of town. **ROUTES** was scrawled at the top of the map in big red letters.

Must be for the postmen, Hamish thought,. *But why would they need to cross the old grey bridge? The only thing beyond that is the cliffs . . .*

Hamish took a step back to get a better look at the map, but as he did so caught a whiff of that smell again. It seemed to lead to the room next door.

Curious, he followed the whiff and pushed open the door.

What he saw inside was something he would sadly never be able to *un*see.

Eeeeeurgh!

Grenville Bile's face was bright red as he sat with his pants around his ankles on a grubby beige toilet. He was straining and sweating and making a dreadful face. His fists were clenched and one hand reached out for a scrappy roll of toilet tissue. His teeth were bared and his belly spilled out, resting across the tops of his legs.

Oh, no. No one needed *that* in their life.

Hamish looked away out of instinct, but then looked back. Grenville had clearly been in the middle of some unfortunate toilet business when the Pause occurred, and looked like he was still only halfway through. What a way to spend the Pause! On the bog!

Hamish decided the right thing to do was simply close the door and leave this boy to his very private goings-on. That would be the right thing to poo.

I mean, *do*.

But, as he began to respectfully back away, Hamish saw the very thing he'd come here for: The Explorer, on Grenville's chubby wrist. And something inside him sparked and burnt for a second. It was a little bit of fury.

Steal my dad's watch, will you? he thought, getting angrier. *Chase me through town? Bop me on the nose? Chuck Colin Robinson in a bush? Throw pencils at everybody? Well . . . who's in charge now, you big red prawn?*

Hamish realised that for the first time he was in complete control of Grenville. He could do anything he wanted.

So he grabbed the roll of toilet paper Grenville was reaching for and he threw it into the hallway. It bounced and rolled away.

'Ha! Try reaching it now!' he said, out loud, and with excitement and confidence rising in his tummy.

Now to get his watch back!

Very carefully, Hamish trod around Grenville and unfastened The Explorer – taking care not to touch anything else at all in that grim and gruesome place. Then he suddenly had another thought.

Quite a cheeky one, in fact.

No, he couldn't do that.

Could he?

No way! That would be a terrible thing to do.

If he did the thing he was thinking of, he'd be no better than Grenville Bile himself . . .

No. He simply could not.

. . .

Might be *fun*, though.

So, very quickly, Hamish kneeled down, grabbed both sides of Grenville's horrible lime-green underpants and heaved them upwards as hard as he could. He managed to get them to Grenville's knees, then did his best to slide them across those two sweaty thighs. And then – with *great* effort and *huge* skill – Hamish whipped them towards Grenville's bottom as hard and fast as he could.

He'd done it! Grenville was wearing his underpants again!

Wearing them on the toilet!

Wearing them on the toilet while *not yet finished*!

Ooh, Hamish did *not* want to be here when Grenville made his final push.

Talking of which . . . he'd better go.

Hamish was still giggling when he pulled the front door of the Bile residence shut again.

He had his watch back. And he'd taken his sweet *Gre*venge.

'So?' came a voice, breaking the absolute silence and causing Hamish to jump out of his skin.

It was Alice Shepherd.

She was leaning on the lamp post opposite with a fishburger in one hand and a lollipop in the other.

'You came to get me?' he said, delighted.

'I came to see if you'd get the watch,' she said. 'To see if you were the kind of boy who'd stand up to his enemies.'

'Well, the Pause made it a bit easier and—'

'And I needed to speak to you. I have some news, Hamish. And a secret. A very big secret. A very big, very horrible secret.'

'What kind of news? What kind of secret?'

'I just *said* it was a very big, very *horrible* one,' she said, impatiently. 'Did you get your watch back?'

Hamish showed it to her, proudly.

'Amazing,' she said. 'What time does it say?'

'6.15.'

'So any second now—'

Flies in the air started to move again. A bird whizzed by. Somewhere a car horn tooted. This girl was *good*!

And suddenly, from inside number nine Knotweed Lane, there was the biggest, most deafening, most confused cry of horror you've ever heard.

'**OOHHHNNNNOOOOOOOO OOOOOOOOOOOO!**' it went. '**MYYY PAAAAAAAAANNNNNTTTS!**'

Hamish put his hands across his mouth. I guess Grenville had realised he suddenly had his pants on again.

Alice frowned and cocked her head.

'What did you do?' she said with a smirk.

And as they began to jog away, all they could now hear was a furious Postmaster.

'**Oh, GRENVILLE!**' she yelled. '**NOT AGAIN, BOY! NOT AGAIN!**'

Vantastic

Alice led Hamish to a clearing in the woods before stopping. Hamish looked around. Why had Alice brought him here?

'What's the secret?' he asked, flustered. 'Can you tell me yet?'

'Shh,' said Alice, listening for something.

There was a large old metal shed to one side of the clearing that had been painted green to blend in with the trees around it. Branches hung low over its roof and a big brass lock stopped intruders from getting inside too easily.

'What is this place?' asked Hamish.

'It was my grandad's secret allotment,' whispered Alice, still with one hand cupped around her ear to listen better. 'This was his tool shed.'

'Why are we here?'

'Because I need you to meet some people,' said Alice, importantly.

And as Hamish was forming his next question . . . he heard music in the distance.

A kind of tinkly-plinkity music.

A sort of plonkety-plunkety music.

Like a very large music box.

What's more, it was getting louder.

Hamish knew that music. Though he'd never heard it played quite like this.

It was the National Anthem.

'Where's that music coming from?' he asked Alice, but as it got louder still, the low purr of an approaching vehicle meant that she didn't need to answer his question.

Through a dark canopy of trees Hamish could make out two bright, square headlights and the engine squeal of an old van. A flashing blue light on its roof lit the trees as it spun.

It couldn't be . . . could it? Yes it was . . . an *ice-cream van*?

Hamish flashed a look of concern at Alice. She nodded her reassurance.

The van slowed to a stop by Hamish's feet and he could see it was being driven by a bespectacled boy no older than he was, who stared at Hamish through the windscreen with a very serious look on his face.

The kid turned the engine off and the music stopped immediately. The back doors burst open and out jumped another boy, a girl and then another boy.

The group saluted Alice. Hamish vaguely recognised a couple of them. One of them was in the year above him at Winterbourne, he thought.

Hamish checked out the ice-cream van. Underneath all the pictures of Knobbly Bobblies and Fabs and 99s was a big round logo: a clenched fist holding an ice-cream cone under the flash of some powerful lightning.

And, under all *that*, the letters:

PDF

'Hamish Ellerby,' said Alice. 'Meet the PDF.'

'The PDF?' said Hamish, as all eyes turned to him.

'Yes,' said Alice. 'This, Hamish . . . is The Pause Defence Force.'

PAUSE
DEFENCE
FORCE

ALICE

PDF MEMBER #: 1

CODENAME: Control.

MOPED: Blue Streak.

DEPARTMENT: Head Office.

SPECIAL SKILLS: A cool head in the face of danger.

SIGNATURE MOVES: The Brow Furrow,
  The Withering Glance, The Elbow Chop.

SECRET FACT: Scared of the dark. But will never,
  ever admit it.

BUSTER

PDF MEMBER #: 2

CODENAME: Muscles.

DEPARTMENT: Innovations and Weapons of Mass
Distraction.

MOPED: Thunderbum.

SPECIAL SKILLS: Super soup-ups. Buster's first tricycle
could do forty-eight miles per hour by the time he'd
finished with it. He fell off it one day and it just kept
going. It was last spotted trundling past John O'Groats
and into the sea.

SIGNATURE MOVE: The Guilty Lizard (no one really
knows what this is).

SECRET FACT: Buster can't keep a secret. Don't tell
anyone. He'll do that himself.

ELLIOT

PDF MEMBER #: 3

CODENAME: Brainbox.

DEPARTMENT: Strategies and Operations. And
Dance.

MOPED: The Professor.

SPECIAL SKILLS: Maps, graphs and knowing a lot
more about things than you do.

SIGNATURE MOVE: The Furious Flying
Foot Stamp.

SECRET FACT: One day, Elliot will go on to become
Prime Minister. Of Sweden.

VENK

PDF MEMBER #: 4

CODENAME: Doesn't need one.

DEPARTMENT: Whatevs.

MOPED: Unnamed

SPECIAL SKILLS: Just being himself, yo.

SIGNATURE MOVE: The Casual Smirk, The Wry
Comment, The Slick Quiff.

SECRET FACT: He *reeeally* wishes he was in a boyband.
He wants to call it *M'agickalGoldenBoyz* and dress all in
denim. Please don't tell his friends (especially Buster).

CLOVER

PDF MEMBER #: 5

CODENAME: The Phantom.

DEPARTMENT: Covert Missions and Black Ops.

MOPED: The Glitter Donkey.

SPECIAL SKILLS: Master of Disguise. Stamp
collecting.

SIGNATURE MOVE: The Now You See Me, Now I'm
Right Behind You Holding a Frying Pan!

SECRET FACT: Can say 'Hello, I need the toilet' in
nine languages. Has never fallen over. For years she
thought her uncle worked for the KGB. It turned out he
worked in a KFC.

21

Pausewalkers Unite!

'You said it was just us!' hissed Hamish, taking Alice to one side once she'd introduced them all. 'You said it was me and you and no one else.'

'I'm sorry,' said Alice, leaning against a tree. 'I wanted to ease you in gently, see if you could handle the truth and hold your own. This is some pretty big stuff we're talking about.'

'So who are this lot?' asked Hamish, pointing at the others.

'They're like you and me. Some of them have parents who vanished. Some of them have parents at home they don't *want* to vanish. But all of them are Pausewalkers.'

Hamish took a breath.

'The more grown-ups that disappear,' he said, quietly, 'the more certain I am that my dad is out there somewhere.'

'Maybe he is,' said Alice. 'But you have to protect yourself too. You have to remember that maybe he isn't.'

Hamish nodded, sadly. He knew she was right.

'Right, so this is how it works,' said Buster, interrupting things. 'I'm in charge of the PDF's van and general transport needs,' he said. 'When a Pause hits, you want to make sure you use every second and have a speedy vehicle!'

Buster had an Afro which almost doubled the size of his head, thick black glasses, some pretty impressive muscles for an eleven-year-old and a little pot belly he nicknamed 'The Beast'.

'The Beast needs feeding!' he'd often yell, apparently.

Lucky he had access to his uncle's old ice-cream van then, eh?

'But it's not just the van, Hamface,' said Buster, who kept getting Hamish's name wrong. In just a few minutes, he'd called him 'Hamface', 'Hedgehog' and 'Hilda'.

Buster pointed behind him. The PDF had had the same idea as Hamish: Mr Slackjaw's beautiful Vespas. 'Check out *The Fleet*!'

'Mr Slackjaw's missing mopeds!' said Hamish. 'You . . . stole them?'

Buster looked horrified.

'*Borrowed*, Harold,' he said, before adding, rather guiltily. 'And . . . modified. Enhanced. *Improved.*'

Hamish took them all in. There was a scooter for each of the team, parked in a line, each on its own stand.

One was jet-black with a bright blues streak down the side. He reckoned he know whose that was.

Next to it was a muddy old scooter that had been painted olive green. It had giant tyres and what looked like an enormous peashooter stuck on the front. That had to be Buster's.

Behind it was another one that was brand new – yellow and red, and covered in big silver stars and lights and bell and whistles.

'That one's mine,' said a blonde-haired girl in a stripy jumper. 'I'm Clover. I'm in charge of reconnaissance.'

'What – *spying*?' said Hamish, a little shocked. 'Doesn't that moped rather . . . stand out?'

'I'm a master of disguise,' she said. 'Watch this. I'm a girl, right?'

Hamish nodded. Clover whipped out a fake moustache from one of her many pockets and stuck it to her upper lip.

'Now I'm a middle-aged bank manager.'

Then she tore the moustache off, turned it on its side and hung it from her chin.

'Now I'm a two-thousand-year-old Japanese emperor.'

Then she very quickly stuck it between the top of her nose and her forehead.

'Now I'm an old lady with a monobrow.'

Everybody applauded.

'Cool,' said Hamish. 'But how come you want to disguise yourself as grown-ups when grown-ups are the very thing the Terribles are after?'

Clover's face fell.

'Yeah, good point,' she said, taking the fake moustache off and screwing it up in her hand.

'I'm Elliot,' said a boy with the biggest brown eyes, framed by two very expressive eyebrows. 'Strategies and Operations.'

'What does that mean?' asked Hamish.

'I'm not entirely sure,' said Elliot, one eyebrow raised quizzically. 'But basically I keep a note of everything we're doing. I help us work out when the next Pause might be and how long it will last. But it's not what I really want to do.'

'What do you really want to do?' asked Hamish.

'I just want to *dance*,' said Elliot, and he did a little jig. 'But apparently that's not very useful in a war.'

Hamish nodded his understanding.

'Because that's what this is,' said the last of the kids, stepping out from the shadows. 'It's a war.'

This kid was quite tall. He had skinny jeans, sunglasses propped up on his forehead, a T-shirt with a skull on it and the look of someone who didn't scare easily.

'I'm Venk,' he said, dramatically. 'Short for Venkatesh. I've seen you around school. You hang out with that nervous kid a lot.'

'Robin,' said Hamish.

'What does *he* make of all this?'

'I'll be honest: I haven't really told him. He once fainted because I told him a friend of mine's cousin's friend's brother's cousin once thought he saw a ghost. I'm not sure what hearing about actual, real-life Terribles would do to him.'

'Fair enough,' said Venk. 'That one's mine, by the way.'

He pointed at a dark purple Vespa with polished chrome spikes all over it. It had been modified so the handles were really high and the seat was really low. On the back was a long springy flagpole supporting a flag that read 'PAUSEWALKERS FOREVER'.

Hamish was impressed.

'I bet that—'

'The girls dig me, yeah,' said Venk. 'You're right.'

'That's not actually what I was going to—'

'It's kind of you to point that out. Cheers, man.'

Alice wrinkled her nose. She didn't seem particularly impressed.

'And what about you, Hamish Ellerby?' said Venk, letting his sunglasses drop from his forehead to his eyes. 'What do you bring to the team? What makes *you* special?'

Hamish thought about it, then held his watch out for them to see.

'I guess you can call me The TimeKeeper.'

Venk smiled.

'Hamish,' said Alice. 'Did you bring your mum's graph like I asked you?'

Hamish pulled out a neatly-folded sheet of A4 paper.

'I found a copy in the wastepaper basket at home,' he said.

'What's that?' asked Elliot, perking up. 'Is that . . .?'

He took it and read it.

'This is gold dust!' he said, delighted.

'And now,' said Alice, as the gang fell silent, 'I can tell you why I brought you all here.'

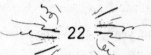

22

The End is Nigh...

So it was *true*.

The Pauses were not just getting longer, and not just getting more and more frequent, but the Pauses were *also* getting more *dangerous*.

At school the next morning, Hamish couldn't stop thinking about the Terribles.

The more they come, the more people they take.

The more people they take, the longer they can stay.

The longer they stay, the more people they can grab.

The more they grab, the less careful they are.

The less careful they are, the quicker they come back.

All of which means they're faster, they're meaner, they're hungrier . . . and they're here.

'So!' said Mr Longblather, eyeing Class 4E, and jolting Hamish from his thoughts. 'I thought today we would talk some more about the wonders of *soil erosion*!'

Hamish sat in his classroom and put his head in his hands,

remembering the night before, his mind was still spinning from all the things the PDF had told him . . .

'Look at your mum's graph!' Elliot had said, holding it up.

'It's just a graph,' Hamish had replied, not sure what the fuss was about.

'No, no!' said Elliot, excited. 'Look at the way the line rises! Very slowly at first, since just before Christmas. Just one or two here or there, but then you start to see it get higher and higher. That means more anger in town! Which means the Terribles must have struck!'

'If we add that information to what we already know,' Alice had added, 'we can see the Terribles are speeding up.'

'And not just speeding up!' Elliot had exclaimed, pointing one finger in the air to look more dramatic. 'But racing towards something!'

Hamish looked blank.

'Everything points,' Elliot had said, 'to there being some kind of Final Event.'

'A Final Event?' Hamish had replied. 'What do you mean, a Final Event?'

'Something cataclysmic,' Elliot said, his eyes burning bright with fear and excitement. 'Something apocalyptic. An event so heinous and awful that it doesn't bear thinking about.

Look at the graph!'

He held it up over the campfire they'd built, so they could see a little better.

'When this red "complaints" line goes straight up in the air – when it's vertical – that's when we can expect something really bad.'

'Why?' asked Buster.

'Because that's the moment when things can't get any worse,' replied Elliot.

'What will happen?' asked Clover, shaken. 'What is this event?'

'The Final Event is when they'll take everybody else,' Elliot had said, grabbing her by the shoulders. 'Men, women, children, teenagers, the lot.'

'Teenagers!' said Clover. 'But how do you know when they've been turned mean? They're always mean!'

'That's the genius of it,' said Elliot. 'They could have been taking teenagers this whole time. No one would know!'

The more they thought about it, the more it made sense. All over Starkley, grown-ups were disappearing at an alarming rate, but no one was doing anything. After all – most people returned after a couple of days and, when someone vanished for longer, everyone just made excuses.

'Oh, he must have gone on holiday,' you'd hear, about the man in the sailor's cap who runs the supermarket, even though he'd never taken a holiday in fifty years.

There were stories about people winning the lottery and suddenly buying a castle in Scotland and getting butlers and a sofa made of gold.

Or that they'd been spotted walking down Starkley High Street and suddenly offered a modelling contract by Lovely Big Nose magazine and whisked off to Milan to be the Next Big Nose.

Or that they'd gone swimming and were enjoying it so much they'd ended up in Calais and just decided to stay.

No one seemed to question anything. It was like the grown-ups who hadn't been taken just didn't know how to deal with how the town was changing.

Hamish snapped out of it and stared out of the classroom window.

Two fat men were arguing over a cat.

A car stopped and a woman rolled her window down and started shouting at the men, using words I just cannot repeat to ears as pure and angelic as yours.

Someone else whizzed by on a bike and knocked the woman's wing mirror off, and the two men started laughing.

So she got out and started chasing them around with a
stale baguette she happened to have in her boot.

The world was noisier. Shoutier. More argument-ier.
Angrier. Snidier. Snippier. Chippier. And really quite
horrible-r.

It. Was. All. Too. Much.

Hamish was going to meet up with the PDF again after
school. Elliot had calculated there was a Pause due tonight.
And now they had to prepare for whenever this terrifying

Final Event might take place too.

Hamish sighed.

Mr Longblather was striding up and down the centre of the classroom, clipping the ear of the odd child here or there if he didn't like the sound of their breathing or thought their posture could be better.

Hamish straightened his back.

Who would be next to go?

He cast a quiet glance around the classroom. It was not quite the usual scene. No one was misbehaving. No one was chatting or passing notes.

'My mum says I should probably stay at home for a while,' whispered Robin suddenly, and this really wasn't like him, taking a risk by talking in class. 'You know how nervous she gets.'

He rolled his eyes, as if he wasn't just as nervous as she was.

'Anyway, she seems to think something really weird is going on. She says she can sense the anger.'

'There *is* something really weird going on,' said Hamish. 'But I just don't know whether to say what it—'

'ELLERBY! YOU ARE TALKING! WHY IS THIS?' was the next thing Hamish heard, followed by a thunk on the side of his head and the smell of chalk in the air once more.

Oh, great. Wednesday detention it was.

Hamish had been given a shopping list of vital items he was told he would need. The kids of the PDF had been working hard these last few weeks.

Wherever they could, and however they could, they were all about scuppering the Terribles and their evil masters, the WorldStoppers.

As he sat in Mr Longblather's detention, he thought again about his new pals in the PDF . . .

'Alice found me about six weeks ago,' Buster had told him. 'She followed my ice-cream van one day. Then together we found the others. We almost didn't find Clover, to be honest.'

'Why?'

'She'd disguised herself as a bush,' he said. 'That's one of her best disguises. Actually, it's her only really good one.'

'And what did you do?' Hamish asked.

'We tried to come up with ways of stopping the Terribles. Elliot tried mixing all sorts of concoctions which he hoped might dissolve them. He'd mix washing-up liquid with battery acid, things like that.'

'And it didn't work?'

'No,' Buster had told him. 'If anything, it just made them look a bit cleaner. And they find battery acid absolutely delicious.'

'What else?'

'We tried trapping them in holes. We tried swatting them with garage doors I'd rigged up to big springs. We tried writing them a convincing note telling them to go home.'

'But they just kept coming,' Venk had added. 'More and more of them were swarming into town. The stink rising over Starkley. Taking more grown-ups every single time.'

'Ideally,' Clover had told him, 'we'd catch one. That way we can prove they exist. If we could catch one and show it to the police or the army or the mayor then maybe they'd do something.'

'What about taking a picture of one?' Hamish had suggested.

'Tried it,' Alice replied. 'The only thing that comes out is whatever was Paused. On every CCTV camera and on every phone.'

And that, Buster had explained, was why Hamish's watch would come in so handy. With The Explorer, the PDF would be able to time the Pauses no matter where in Starkley they were – not just if they were near the town clock. They would be able to see how far into a Pause they were – and work out how long they had left before the world started up again.

203

This, Elliot determined, would be very handy indeed.

Because it was down to them to stop the Terribles from reaching the Final Event.

As he walked away from school, Hamish studied the blue canvas satchel Venk had given him the night before.

It was a PPP – a Pause Protection Pack. It made Hamish's PDK look a little amateur.

It had the international symbol for 'pause' and 'PPP' sprayed on it.

And now Hamish had a list of things he needed to fill it.

TABASCO HOT SAUCE and AFTERSHAVE SPRAYER

'To the Terribles, humans absolutely stink,' said Venk. 'But they love our stink. That's why they lick us and paw at us, and put their little sucker cups all over us. A few sprays of extra-strength Tabasco hot sauce from an old perfume or aftershave bottle and they're not going to do it again in a hurry!'

ONE PAIR OF MARMITE GLOVES

'You don't want to leave your stink anywhere,' said Clover. 'It's always best to cover our tracks, especially if you're on spying duty. Marmite gloves keep them from sniffing our handprints!'

ONE PACK MIXED SWEETS FROM MADAME COUS COUS'S INTERNATIONAL WORLD OF TREATS

'For vital sustenance during the Pause!' said Buster. 'You like sweets, don't you, Hotdog?' 'It's Hamish,' said Hamish. 'Of course it is,' said Buster. 'Sorry, Hellfish.'

ONE SMALL BOTTLE OF HYGIENE GEL

'For immediate application following contact with a Terrible!' said Alice, pulling a face.

And finally . . .

ONE MAP OF STARKLEY

'For obvious reasons!' said Venk. (And if you can't work out why they'd need a map, maybe you don't belong in the PDF! If so, put this book down before someone calls the authorities.)

Looking at the list, the only thing that would be tricky was the bag of sweets, considering Hamish was still banned from Madame Cous Cous's International World of Treats. And just as he was working out if a bag of sweets from somewhere else might do, Hamish noticed something unusual happening down an alleyway to his right.

It was Grenville Bile.

He was being pushed up against a wall by two much bigger kids.

And for once Grenville looked afraid.

Was it possible? Was the bully being bullied?

'I thought you wanted to show us your new watch!' Hamish heard the bigger of the two big kids growl.

'Oh,' said Grenville, quaking. 'Yeah, I do. It's just—'

'What?' said the boy. 'It's just that you were *lying* about it?'

Hamish felt in his pocket to make sure The Explorer was still there.

'No!' said Grenville. 'I wasn't lying! I had a new watch! It was really cool, like I said! It's just I, um, well . . .'

'Sure,' said the second big boy. 'We believe you. This must be totally different from all those other times you said you had something and then didn't.'

'Yeah! Like the time you said David Beckham might be picking you up from school.'

'Yeah!' said the second big boy. 'We waited hours!'

The boys picked Grenville up by the scruff of his neck, which was no mean feat given the size of it.

'I told you, he missed his bus!' said Grenville, lying desperately. 'And I honestly have all that other stuff I told you about.'

'Of course you do,' said the second bigger boy, grinning, sickeningly. 'You know what, Grenville Bile? You're just a worthless little groat. Prepare for this week's punishment.' He raised one huge, meaty fist. Grenville shut his eyes and whimpered.

This week's punishment? thought Hamish. Did this happen every week? Hamish had never heard Grenville whimper before. And now he was about to get beaten up!

Part of him wanted to watch the little bully get his just

desserts. But, after the underpants prank, Hamish had already had his revenge. And what was happening here just seemed *unfair*.

'Oh, hello, Grenville!' said Hamish, waving confidently and striding forward.

Grenville opened one piggy eye and squinted to see who was coming. His face fell. He thought Hamish would love this. The bully getting what he deserved.

'Hey,' said Hamish. 'You forgot your watch at school.'

He took The Explorer out from his pocket. It glinted in the sun. The two bigger boys stared at it, then at Hamish, then at Grenville.

'It's super cool, Grenville,' said Hamish. 'You're really lucky.'

'Oh, er . . . yeah, cheers, Hamish,' said Grenville, silently wondering why his old enemy was helping him. 'Thank you for bringing my watch that is definitely mine back to me.'

One of the bigger boys sniffed. 'Huh,' he said. 'Well, just because you're telling the truth about a watch—'

'Oh, and Grenville,' said Hamish, 'thank you so much again for letting me come round yesterday and see your complete set of Super Action Rascals.'

'Oh, um, that's okay, Hamish,' said Grenville, slowly.

'And your massive telly and your film collection, and all your movie posters. And your pool table.'

The two big bullies stared at Grenville, surprised.

'And your table football table,' Hamish continued, walking closer. 'And your original pinball machine, and your games consoles, and your solid gold top hat.'

The bullies were staring at Hamish now, but he wasn't scared. Hamish knew what real fear was these days, and a couple of thick old bullies wasn't it.

'And your train track,' Hamish said, starting to enjoy himself, 'and your radio-controlled cars and your fish tanks, and your massive stuffed raccoon.'

'Yes, fine, not a problem,' said Grenville, thinking that was probably enough now.

'And your life-sized cardboard cut-outs of the Prime Minister,' said Hamish, improvising. 'And your replica football stadium, your moon rocks and, of course, thank you SO much for letting me see your personal robot-monkey butler.'

Too much?

Apparently not, because the two bigger boys cleared their throats, gave Grenville an apologetic pat on the back and began to walk away. They'd be leaving Grenville alone for a while, Hamish suspected. If only because they were probably worried he'd set his personal robot-monkey butler on them.

'Um . . . thanks, Hamish,' said Grenville, very sincerely and rubbing his neck.

Hamish held the palm of his hand out.

Grenville dropped The Explorer into it.

'I'm sorry about taking it off you,' he said. 'Those boys, they . . . well, they think unless you've got money you're a nobody. They've been giving me a hard time for months. I don't have all those toys, Hamish. But I guess I got used to pretending.'

You know what would have been the best thing in the world for Hamish to say right at this moment? Probably something like, 'Well, I guess we've all learned an important lesson today.'

Or, 'We all make mistakes. It's forgiveness that sets us apart.'

Or, 'Money is not what makes the world go round, Grenville!'

Or anything else that you might see on an inspirational bumper sticker, really.

He'd have looked so wise. And I think both you and I

would really have felt like he'd been on some kind of personal journey and all our lives were the richer for it.

But Hamish wasn't a 'big moment' kind of kid, so instead he just said, 'That's okay, Grenville!' followed by, 'Hey! I *saw you on the toilet yesterday*!'

And then he ran away laughing, finally feeling his revenge was complete, while Grenville stood there fuming.

'You're late,' said Alice, grumpily as Hamish approached the clearing.

'I had detention,' said Hamish. 'Actually, the whole class did. And the class next door. And Mr Longblather got so furious with himself that he ended up giving himself detention too, so we had to wait for him to finish that before he could come and supervise ours. And, after detention, I had a score to settle with an old nemesis. And sort out my PPP.' It had actually been quite a busy day now he thought about it.

'Nice,' said Alice. 'But while you've been out there, having fun and settling scores and going shopping, Elliot's been working hard with Mr Bodfish.'

'Who's he?'

'Head of maths at St Autumnal's. Elliot showed him your

mum's graph. He changed all the words and pretended it was a graph that shows how often birds poop on his dad's car. And Mr Bodfish came to a conclusion.'

'What was it?'

'That Elliot's dad should move his car.'

'Oh. And what else?'

'He found a pattern in the numbers,' she said. 'He was able to work out when they will reach their peak. That means when the Final Event will be.'

'What are you saying?' asked Hamish, urgently. 'That we know? That there will *be* a Final Event *and* when it's coming?'

'Oh, Hamish,' she said, putting one hand on his shoulder. 'We've got until Saturday. That's three days. And, after that, the world as we know it will change forever.'

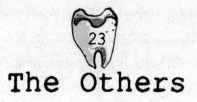

The Others

'Three days,' said Elliot, shaking his head, and tapping the graph. 'And only three potential Pauses in between.'

'It's not enough,' said Venk, worried. 'Three days is not enough!'

In the clearing, each member of the PDF had a Pause Protection Pack over one shoulder.

Hamish was wearing his 'H' jumper as usual. The rest were mainly in overalls.

Hamish checked The Explorer.

'What time is the next Pause?' he asked.

'Around 7.04,' said Elliot, checking his workings. 'Though remember, I can't tell you *exactly* when.'

It was 7 o'clock now.

'What I want to know is – why us?' said Hamish.

'What do you mean?' asked Venk.

'Well – why are *we* the only Pausewalkers? What links us?'

Everyone thought about it. Venk toyed with the strap of his PPP.

'Well, we're all kids,' he said, shrugging. 'Of about the same age. And we all live in Starkley.'

'Yes,' said Hamish. 'That's true. But there must be something else. There must be a reason.'

'We go to different schools,' said Clover. 'So it's not that. Hey – maybe it's our birthdays! I was born on July 2nd – what about you?'

'January 10th,' said Buster.

'November 22nd,' said Venk.

Hmmm. Well, it wasn't that either.

Hamish checked his watch again. 7.02.

'Aha!' said Venk, having an idea. 'I'm the eldest child in my family!'

'Me too!' said Buster, delighted.

'Me three!' said Clover.

Were they onto something?

'But I'm the youngest,' said Elliot.

'Me too,' said Hamish.

'Me three,' said Alice.

They fell into silence, thinking hard. The truth was, they were all pretty different.

'There has to be *something*,' said Hamish.

'Ow,' said Buster, rubbing his cheek.

'What's up with you?' asked Alice.

'It's nothing,' said Buster. 'I think my filling's coming loose.'

'You eat too many sweets,' she said. 'Feeding that Beast of yours.'

'You can talk,' he replied. 'You pretty much have a lollipop on your person twenty-four hours a day!'

'It's Chomps for me,' said Hamish, smiling. 'Or it was, until I was banned from—'

'Ow ow *ow*!' said Buster again. His tooth really was killing him.

'You should get another filling,' said Venk, helpfully.

'Oh, sure,' said Buster. 'I'll just do that myself tonight, shall I?'

'You should go to my dentist, Dr Fussbundler at The Tooth Hurts,' said Hamish. He checked his watch. It was 7.04. He looked around. No sign of the Pause.

'I did go to The Tooth Hurts,' said Buster. 'Dr Fussbundler glurged this great glug of globby goo all over my gums. He wouldn't stop making awful dentist jokes.'

'Yes!' said Clover. 'I've noticed that when I go. "I'm *filling* good today!" and all that. I couldn't stop groaning on my last visit.'

'Wait,' said Hamish. 'Wait just a second . . .'

'And then he looms over you, doesn't he?' said Venk, laughing. 'And he says—'

'"*Brace* yourself!"' chuckled Alice, rolling her eyes.

'Wait!' said Hamish, again, and everyone turned to him, slightly annoyed he was interrupting their fun.

'*You've* had a filling at Dr Fussbundler's,' he said, pointing at Buster. 'And so have *you*, and *you*, and *you*, and *you* . . .'

'Yes?' said Alice.

'And so have *I*.'

'So?'

'So maybe that's what links us!'

'What – too many sweets?' said Buster.

It was like a lightbulb above Hamish's head.

'The fillings!' he said. 'I think the *fillings* stop us from being affected by the Pause!'

Revolution
Revelation

This was a revelation.

And the kids had realised something super, super quickly.

They couldn't be the only kids in Starkley to have had a filling. That would be madness. How could Dr Fussbundler pay for such nice white walls if they were the only customers? How could Madame Cous Cous survive if she wasn't selling enough sweets to rot children's teeth?

No. There must be other kids who'd had that grey gunk slathered on their teeth by Eric Fussbundler. And that meant there would be other Pausewalkers out there.

Hamish knew immediately that this was important.

'We can raise an army!' he said.

'Sure,' said Venk. 'In three days.'

'We'll break into The Tooth Hurts,' said Alice. 'There should be a record of all the kids who've had fillings in town. Then we can just go round, door to door. We'll recruit them to the PDF!'

And that was when Buster stepped forward.

'Or in the twenty-six minutes and twenty-six seconds of this Pause,' he said, 'there may be another way.'

At the very, very top of the very, very highest rollercoaster at the funfair, all six kids had crammed themselves into the very front carriage.

'The Gap-toothed Otter!' said Hamish, happily. 'We meet again!'

This had always been Hamish's favourite ride. That's why he saved all year to make sure he could go on it again and again. An enormous, spindly rollercoaster with a giant plaster otter's head at the bottom. His dad had introduced him to it and said it even used to come to Starkley when *he* was a kid. There was a space in the middle of the otter's two enormous front teeth for you to shoot through at high speed. Elliot had already been sick twice and all they'd done was climb to the top.

Buster pressed 'Stop' on the remote control he'd rigged up.

'My dad was an engineer,' he said, as the carriage teetered at the peak. 'I used to practise for hours in his garage.'

'Was he taken too?' said Hamish. 'Is your dad out there in the woods somewhere?'

The group fell quiet.

'No,' said Buster, sadly. 'No, he wasn't taken.'

'Oh,' said Hamish, realising what Buster was saying. 'Oh, Buster, I'm sorry. I didn't know.'

Now Hamish could guess why Buster was so determined. Buster just wanted to make the world a bit better.

It was easy to see why, sitting at the top of this rollercoaster, looking out over Starkley at night. You could see everything from up here. You could see the town clock. You could see Grenville's house. You could see the top of Hamish's roof. You could see Winterbourne, and St Autumnal's, and Spring Grove primary, and the Summer House nursery. You could see it all.

The Pause had frozen the town at a beautiful time of night.

'This seems quite an unfair punishment for poor toothbrush technique,' said Elliot, sadly. 'Being stuck in the Pause.'

Hamish hadn't thought about it that way. He saw it differently. He saw it as an opportunity.

'I guess I'm just scared,' admitted Elliot. 'The first time it happened, I was just stuck there at breakfast, with my family. I'd just made a joke about particle physics in relation to quantum mechanics and they all froze. It was like they just didn't *enjoy* jokes about particle physics in relation to quantum mechanics!'

'Weird,' said Alice.

'Anyway,' said Elliot, 'three minutes later, they all started eating again like nothing had happened. From that moment, I just felt a bit disconnected from them. Like they were one thing and I was another.'

'You're just like them,' said Hamish, reassuringly. 'You're still one of them. It's just that at the same time, you're different too. Maybe you've got a chance to help them. *Protect* them. Protect the world! Prevent the Final Event!'

Out of the blue, Hamish's dad's words came to him . . .

'Prevention's as good as a cure, H! Always prepare!'

Then . . .

'Look!' Alice said. 'You were right, Buster! Movement!'

Somewhere far below, a tubby lad in a stripy top darted nervously around, scurrying about and checking the bins.

'I know that kid! His name's Dexter,' said Alice. 'He's scavenging. Maybe they got his parents.'

'And over there – look!' cried Buster. 'There's a girl, down there. They can join us!'

The girl, who was maybe eleven years old, was carrying a vast, teetering tower of pizza boxes.

'She's not eating all that on her own,' said Elliot. 'There must be even more. Even more Pausewalkers!'

'Yes!' they all yelled, high-fiving and slapping each other on the back, and smiling and laughing and stopping very suddenly when they heard ... **VVVAAAAAAA AAAAAAAAAAARRRRRR**.

'That wasn't me,' said Buster, with a guilty look on his face.

'Oh, no,' said Alice, the blood draining from her face. 'The Bugle.'

'It's a *Terrible* Pause,' said Venk, nervously. 'I thought this wouldn't be a Terrible Pause, Elliot?'

'They must be going even faster than we thought.' said Elliot, pulling the graph from his PPP and examining it. 'We need to get down. Right now. We're sitting ducks up here!'

'We can't get down!' cried Clover. 'They'll notice a rollercoaster screeching about.'

'What do we do?' said Elliot. 'What do we do!'

They were *trapped* – ninety metres in the air!

Everyone looked at Alice. She was always the one with the answers, but for the first time since they'd met, Hamish saw she looked lost.

'Alice?' said Elliot, but she was struggling to find the words.

'We *wait*,' said Hamish, taking control. 'We keep still, we keep quiet and we hope they don't look up.'

From the very peak of the ride, the gang watched in horror as the Terribles emerged in greater numbers than ever before.

Out of the woods they poured, seeping into town. From up here, it looked like an ever-thickening oil spill – a horrid black liquid filling in every road and crack in town, like rancid fat slickering into the town's veins.

'They're after someone,' said Hamish, his heart fluttering slightly. 'A grown-up.'

KABLAAAAAANNG!

The rollercoaster began to shake.

'What was that?' asked Venk.

KABLAAAAAAANG!

The great metal structure began to creak and shriek.

It started to judder and shudder.

Venk craned his neck to peer over one side.

'Oh . . .' he said.

'What?' said Clover.

'Oh, dear . . .' said Venk.

'WHAT?' said everybody.

Venk turned to them.

'One's coming up,' he said, looking like he couldn't believe it. 'One's coming up right now!'

'Coming up where?' said Elliot. 'Coming up *here*?'

Buster covered his mouth with his hands then screamed. It sounded like a tiny mouse squeaking in a box.

Panic was setting in. Venk began to tug at the safety bar.

'We need to spray ourselves!' said Buster, opening up his PPP. 'We need some hot sauce!'

'No,' said Hamish. 'If we all stink of hot sauce, the Terrible might work it out. It's too obvious. Look, I've done this before,' He turned to face them all. 'Just stay still. Look blank. Or pretend you're mid-scream. We're on a rollercoaster, after all – if it sees us, we should *look* like we're scared. So look convincing!'

It was the only plan they had. Everyone immediately pulled a ridiculous face. Buster looked like he had constipation. Clover looked like she'd stubbed her toe. Venk looked like he'd been told his feet had just fallen off.

SHUNK

The whole rollercoaster bent to the right!

CREEEEEEEEEEEAAAAAAAAAAAAAK

What if the entire thing toppled over?

SHUUUUNK

It was bending to the left now.

THRAKAAAASH!

One nasty hand slapped over the railings. The gang all held their breath.

THRAKASH!

Another hand slapped over, and four huge and scratchy fingers felt around for something to grip onto.

Then *heeeeeave* . . . the great beast appeared.

This was not a Terrible any of the PDF had seen before. It had small slits for eyes and pincers where its nose should have been. Its cloak pulled back slightly to reveal a stomach covered in oily fat suckers.

If anyone could have screamed, that would have been the

233

moment they chose. This thing was the grossest, ugliest, worstest thing they'd yet seen!

It clambered and flolloped over the children, planting one horrible foot in Hamish's lap and one wet hand on Venk's disgusted face, before moving down the rollercoaster car, heaving its horrid, flabby, slimy body past each child's face.

Eeewwww!

But it didn't seem to suspect that these were anything other than six ordinary, boring, stinky Starkley children, frozen in time.

'It's gone right past us,' whispered Elliot through the corner of his mouth.

'It's not us it's interested in,' Hamish hissed back. 'Look.'

The Terrible was sitting on the edge of the rollercoaster tracks now, facing the town. It was on its haunches, snuffling and grunting and scratching like a dog.

'It's looking at the clock,' whispered Alice.

Her eyes widened as the Terrible pulled something out from deep within its cloak, and . . .

FVVVAAAAAAA AAAAAAAAAAAAAAAAAAAA

AAAAAAAARRRRRRRR!

Oh my goodness – this was the Bugler! It was warning the rest of the Terribles!

FVVVAAAAAAAAAAAAARRRRRRR!

The power of the Bugle was enormous – the kids' hair all blew to the front of their heads. Venk's ears flapped in the wind.

Down below, hundreds of Terribles began to thunder away, leaving the town, some on their Requines, others billowing through Starkley on foot, their cloaks flapping behind them at speed.

They need to see the clock, thought Hamish, as the smallest brother of a cousin of a smell of a hint of a rumour of an idea began to form in his mind. *One of them always needs to keep its eye on the clock.*

Minutes later, after the Flash, and they'd watched each and every Terrible bound back to wherever they came from, Buster clicked 'Go' on his rollercoaster controller again, taking them back to the bottom of the ride.

Pale, sweaty and with wobbly legs, the PDF were so grateful to be back on solid ground.

'Come on,' said Buster, rather shaken. 'I'll drop you all off at home.'

The ride back into the heart of Starkley was silent. Each of the kids was wearing one of Clover's fake moustaches so that anyone who spotted them might just think a strange family of tiny adults was taking a ride in an ice-cream van. Hamish stared out of the window. The Terribles hadn't even been careful to leave things as they found them this time. Bins had been flipped over. Windows were chipped and cracked. A car had been spun onto its roof. There was rubbish all over the streets. A few unprocessed grown-ups stood around, pointing at them, noticing what had happened but unable to work out how. The PDF stayed low in their seats as they passed.

'If the Terribles are getting this careless,' said Alice, 'that means they're not as bothered about being found out.'

No one needed to point out that this was not a good sign. It could only mean that something big was on the cards. The Final Event was drawing closer. And there were only two Pauses to go.

Hamish jumped out at number thirteen Lovelock Close and waved the gang off.

It had been quite a night and all he wanted to do now was get inside, eat a hot meal and go straight to bed.

But, as he turned round, he noticed something unusual about his house.

All the lights were off.

He frowned.

'Hello?' he said, pushing open the front door. 'Mum? Jimmy?'

He stood in the doorway and listened. There was no answer.

'Jimmy . . . James!' he shouted, now with a slight quiver in his voice. 'Mum?'

He started to feel very uneasy indeed.

And as he walked into the living room and noticed the wide-open French doors, and the spilled cup of tea by the armchair, and the chocolate Mustn'tgrumbles scattered across the floor . . .

Hamish Ellerby realised the terrible, terrible truth.

25

Taken!

They had been taken.

Mum and Jimmy. Jimmy and Mum. Gone.

Hamish had checked every room twice, and then a third time, though his heart grew heavy as he realised it was pointless.

He'd watched the Terribles storm into Starkley. He'd seen with his own eyes as they undertook their dreadful mission. He'd even said, 'They're after someone' as he sat there, in that rollercoaster carriage, trapped and powerless to do anything – not knowing they were after his own family.

What if this was revenge? Maybe the Terribles knew for sure he was a Pausewalker and were looking for him?

Hamish closed the French doors, locked them, tidied up the biscuits, put the spilled teacup on the drainer by the sink and sat down right in the middle of the sofa.

This was Jimmy's seat. He never normally let Hamish sit here.

Well, that was one upside of this whole kidnapping business, he supposed. He could sit wherever he liked.

Hamish stayed there a moment more, then shifted guiltily to the left.

He checked his watch. It was really late, but he didn't want to go to bed. And he didn't want to sleep here.

He knew exactly where to go.

'Taken?' said Alice, shocked, closing her door behind her. 'Oh, Hamish – I'm so sorry.'

Hamish noticed Alice had painted her whole house dark grey, except for the bannisters and door frames and ceilings and floors, which were all electric blue.

'Your parents will go crazy when they see what you've done to your house!' he said.

'I don't think home decor is at the top of their worries,' she said.

'Look – we need to do something,' he said, because he'd made a decision on the long dark walk to Viola Road. 'If we're right and we only have two Pauses left . . . then we need to take the fight to the Terribles.'

He made an important face.

'We need to be *clever*, Hamish,' said Alice.

'I spend my whole life trying to be clever,' said Hamish, walking through to the kitchen and opening the fridge. There was just row after row of fishburgers. 'I'm always trying to do the polite thing and the right thing and usually it gets me chased or beaten up or thrown in a bush with my watch stolen. Maybe for once I want to *start* the fight.'

'So what's your idea?' she said, quietly, as he sniffed a fishburger and put it straight back. On the fridge were the usual signs of family life. Photos of Alice and her family. Drawings. A certificate that read 'Starkley Under-12s

100-metre champion – Alice Shepherd'. A voucher for one per cent off their next pizza delivery order.

'Well,' he said, turning, ready to reveal his big idea. 'I think I should let the Terribles kidnap me.'

Alice raised her eyebrows.

'You should let the Terribles kidnap you,' she repeated.

'I should let the Terribles kidnap me, yes,' he said.

'And then what?'

'Well, then they'll take me to their lair. And that's my plan.'

'That's your plan? That's a terrible plan. What are you going to do when you're in their lair?'

Hamish thought about it.

'Fight them?' he said.

'Fight them. In their own lair, wherever that is? Just you? What are you going to do? Challenge them at Boggle?'

'Well . . . I haven't worked it *all* out yet. I've just got the essence of the plan. But I guess that's when you all turn up in the ice-cream van.'

Alice just stared at him.

'Except!' he said, having a new idea. 'Except Buster can do some cool modifications to the ice-cream van to make it a sort of *battle* ice-cream van.'

'I see . . .' said Alice, filling up a glass at the sink. 'A battle ice-cream van.'

'And . . . you know . . . you've brought a whole army of kids with you and that's when we say, "Hey, Terribles – why are you such a massive bunch of berks?" And *that's* when we take them out.'

Alice put a glass of squash down on the table for Hamish. He clearly needed one.

'We take them out,' she repeated. 'What – for dinner and dancing?'

'No – I mean, we DESTROY THEM!' said Hamish, bringing his fist down on the table with a **BANG** that spilled a bit of his drink. 'Oh, gosh, sorry about that. I'll tidy it up.'

Alice stood and walked to the window.

'I don't think we can destroy them,' she said, slowly. 'I really don't.'

Deep down, Hamish knew that she was right. He'd just been so full of anger and helplessness when he found Mum and Jimmy had gone that all he wanted to do was come up with *something*.

Anything.

Alice stood by the window, silently staring out into the

darkness, while Hamish considered his situation.

First there was his dad. Hamish missed his dad. He missed him more than ever. And now that Mum and Jimmy had been taken, the only person he wanted to speak to was his dad. He'd know what to do. He'd have a plan. It would be a brilliant plan. An incredible one, full of action and bravery and intrigue and rescue. They'd wear matching T-shirts and be an amazing father-and-son team, swapping witty chit-chat as, together, they got Mum and Jimmy back. Of *course* they would.

But Dad was gone.

With the Terribles? Maybe.

Or maybe there was the thought that came to Hamish in the depths of the night. The thought he would always try to drive away and squish. The thought that maybe his dad was just in some other town, hanging out with some other little boy. Making another family laugh each night. Sitting down for dinner and ruffling his new kid's hair. Playing Boggle with him at the kitchen table. Starting afresh, while Hamish's life fell apart.

I mean – what was more likely? That, or world-stopping monsters?

He needed his dad, he knew he did. And with him not

here, what amazing plan had Hamish come up with?

Get kidnapped and call the Terribles berks.

Oh, what was the point? What was the point in fighting? The Terribles were going to win. They always were. Might as well just stay home, like Robin and his family. Might as well just sit back and let it happen. Just let the next two Pauses happen and surrender.

'You've given me an idea,' said Alice, quite suddenly.

26

Action Stations

'I don't understand,' said the small pudgy kid with cheeks like a hamster. 'Can you explain the idea again?'

'Okay,' said Alice, putting her hands on her hips. 'But this will literally be like the three-hundredth time.'

Hamish looked out into the clearing. He couldn't believe it.

Yesterday there had been six of them.

This morning there were *dozens*.

At least twenty-five children, sitting cross-legged on the floor of the wood, outside Alice's grandad's shed.

'I'll go a bit slower this time . . .' she said.

It was late morning the next day and Hamish, Alice, Buster, Elliot, Clover and Venk had been up for hours already.

This was not a day for school. This was a day for *action*.

Here is precisely what had happened.

At exactly 9.01 a.m. Buster had distracted Dr Fussbundler

with his sore filling while Clover crept into the back office
of The Tooth Hurts.

In there, she'd found Dr Fussbundler's records – and now
they had a list of every kid in Starkley who'd had a filling
with that weird **ZINOXYCLUMP™** stuff.

That meant they had a list of every potential Pausewalker
in town.

At 9.04 a.m. that precious list was with the rest of the
PDF.

And by 9.15 a.m. that morning Venk, Alice, Hamish, Clover, Elliot and a slightly sore Buster had split up and made sure Winterbourne and St Autumnal's were completely covered.

'Pssst!' they'd say, from around a corner or behind some bins, whenever they spotted one of Dr Fussbundler's patients. 'Could we possibly have a quick word about the future of life on Earth?'

Now at 11.48 a.m. on an otherwise normal Thursday,

every kid in Starkley who'd been **ZINOXYCLUMP™**-ed was here.

They may not have looked like much – but Hamish could see something special: now they had an army.

There was Darcy and Lola, the twin girls who lived down the road from Clover. They'd been so pleased to discover there was an uprising planned.

Over there by the tree were Finch and Jude and Cody.

And there was Drake and Kit and Rufus, sitting attentively with Ed, Daisy, Mo and Poppy.

Hamish even saw Dexter, the kid in the stripy top they'd seen from high up on the rollercoaster the night before. He'd tried to talk to him, but Dexter remained completely silent, like a boy who'd seen a ghost. He was deathly pale and trembly to the touch, and tried his best simply to hide among everyone else.

Hamish and the PDF stood before these kids, wearing their overalls and some little sergeant patches that Elliot had ironed on to make them look like they were properly in charge. He'd also typed out his very own list of Frequently Asked Questions in a posh font and printed it out on little bits of yellow card, because he thought it might be handy.

He called it a PDFAQ.

~ Elliot's PDFAQ ~

Look. What on Earth is going on?
Good question.
It seems we're being invaded by Terribles
who pause time and somehow we're the
world's first line of defence.

What?
Yes. And tomorrow night is the night of
the Final Event. A fearsome feeding frenzy
that will destroy Starkley forever and
mark the beginning of a global
Terrible takeover!

Sounds awful.
Where do these 'Terribles'
come from?
Either the sea, space or France. At the
moment, our best guess is space, but none
of us has ever been to France, so who
knows what goes on there?

Why have they chosen Starkley?

Because it's so boring and hardly anyone comes here. That means no pesky outsiders and no one ever guessing that something like this could go on here. Plus, it's handy for the sea and there's a twenty-four hour minimart just down by the garage.

When do these fearsome beasts attack?

Look, all we know is they're coming more often, and staying for longer. At first, they came under cover of darkness. Then at about suppertime. Now they're so confident of victory they come day or night. See my graph for further information (diagram 1).

So there's no logic to their appearances?

Why are you looking for logic? Space aliens are stopping the world so they can steal grown-ups, while a group of ten-year-olds with questionable dental hygiene motor about on vehicles they are not qualified to drive in order to hatch a plan to prevent the end of life on Earth as we know it!

Okay. Don't get snarky.
I'm not getting snarky. I'm just saying.

Well, you sound a bit snarky to me.
Well, I'm very sorry, but the pressure is getting to me a bit.

Is that why you've started talking to yourself?
Quite possibly, yes, it is! Good point, Elliot!

Thank you, Elliot.
Okay, this has gone weird.

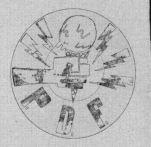

'Where's Buster?' asked Hamish, scanning the crowd of Starkley kids.

'He said he had to pick something up from town,' said Alice. 'But people want more details, Hamish. They're scared.'

'I'll try and explain,' said Hamish, stepping forward and taking a deep breath. All eyes were upon him. He cleared his throat.

'Kids of Starkley,' he said. 'You may have grown up thinking that this was Britain's Fourth Most Boring Town. But it is anything but. In fact, it is at the centre of the most exciting thing that has ever happened in the world ever. The WorldStoppers are upon us. They have sent the Terribles to take away the grown-ups and return them as mean. In less than forty-eight hours, their plan is to finish off Starkley and then start on the rest of the world. And only we can stop them.'

One lone hand shot up.

'But how?' said a girl with her hair in a plait. 'There's nothing about that in the FAQ!'

'*PDFAQ*,' corrected Elliot.

'How are we going to get our parents back?' she wailed. 'How are we going to stop people being mean? We're just kids!'

'We're not just kids,' said Hamish. 'We're *Pausewalkers*.'

A hubble-bubble of chitter-chatter broke out. There was fear in the air. What did this mean? What could *they* possibly do?

'Alice has an idea,' said Hamish, quietening everyone down. 'There's a Pause today, and she thinks there could be a way of beating these WorldStoppers once and for all and getting everything back to normal.'

He stepped back.

'Alice?' he said.

'When there's a Pause,' she said, 'humans stop, right?'

Everyone mumbled their agreement.

'But the Terribles keep moving. And just when the Pause is nearly over, they all run away again. Why?'

'Because they don't want to be seen!' shouted a kid who for some reason was dressed as a ninja.

'Maybe,' said Alice. 'But why are they bothered about being seen? They're so powerful. And most of the grown-ups have either been taken or they're back and they're mean. So maybe they're running away for another reason.'

'What reason?' asked a gangly boy near the back.

'Well – and this is just a guess – I think that when *we* move about, *they* stop still.'

The whole clearing fell silent as the assembled kids thought about what Alice had said.

'What?' shouted someone in the middle.

'What if they have to abide by the same rules?' she went on. 'What if that's why one of them watches the town clock, because if they're still here in Starkley when the Pause finishes, they all just stop?'

Well, it was an idea all right. And what if it was true? Maybe that *was* why the Terribles all panicked and bounded away so quickly when the world was about to return to normal. They were scared of getting frozen! And if the kids could make all the Terribles freeze in time, well . . . they could do as Clover had said and call the police, or the army, or the mayor and say – look! Monsters! It's true! Take them away!

'This seems quite a risk,' said Venk, chipping in. 'But right now it's the only idea that we have. And I, for one, am in.'

'So who's with us?' asked Hamish, and for a moment no one moved.

But then slowly . . .

'I'm in,' yelled Finch, raising one clenched fist in the air.

'We are too!' yelled Lola and Darcy.

'And us!' cried Ed and Rufus.

'And I will help also,' came one last voice, in an odd, stilted accent, from somewhere near the back.

Everybody turned to see from where this low and confident statement had come.

Standing next to Buster was a bulky boy in an ill-fitting T-shirt wearing a bright green Mexican wrestling mask.

'El Gamba is here to helpa!' shouted Grenville Bile, who hadn't really cracked his Mexican accent yet.

'What's the Prawn doing here?' said Alice, wide-eyed, as Hamish put his hands on his hips. 'When did *he* become a Pausewalker?'

'About half an hour ago,' said Buster. 'When we were stealing the list from Dr Fussbundler's, we forgot to check his appointment book. I nipped back and the first thing I saw was Grenville walking out with a brand-new filling. He was already on his way to the sweet shop!'

'Hello?' came another new voice, as a kid pushed his way through the bracken. 'What are we doing? What is this, hide-and-seek?'

It was Robin! He was holding a lollipop from The Tooth Hurts. So *he'd* been there too!

'Robin!' yelled Hamish. 'But I thought your dental hygiene was second to none?'

Robin blushed.

'I may have exaggerated,' he said. 'I'm a little partial to an Austrian Aniseed . . . so what's all this about?'

'Well,' said Hamish, looking awkward, 'I think the answer might shock you a bit.'

'Doubt it,' said Grenville, shrugging. 'Not much shocks me.'

'IT PROBABLY WILL,' said literally everybody else in unison.

'Well, whatever it is, we're in,' replied Grenville, slapping Robin on the back, which seemed to really startle him.

'Then we're ready,' said Hamish, in his best, most heroic voice, as he looked out over this new group of brave friends and time warriors. 'Let us begin . . .'

27

Training Day

Hamish wandered around the clearing proudly while the kids set to work.

They'd filled Grenville and Robin in as gently as they could.

Grenville had taken it remarkably well.

And, once he'd stopped fainting and being sick everywhere, Robin even managed to nod once or twice, before being sick and fainting again.

Grenville had also worked something out, which wasn't like Grenville at all.

'My mum,' he said gently. 'She must have been taken and returned. I want her back to how she was. Before she swapped all my toys for a book about tractors! She used to be good, Hamish. I did too.'

Hamish was pleased Grenville was here. He'd seen a different side of him lately. And not just his *back*side. He was even more pleased that Grenville had found a reason to fight. *No* child deserves to be made to read a book about tractors.

Not even you.

Meanwhile, the rest of the Pausewalkers had split into different groups for what Buster called 'Pause Preparation' (or PP).

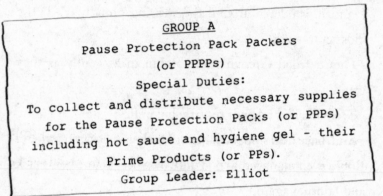

GROUP A
Pause Protection Pack Packers
(or PPPPs)
Special Duties:
To collect and distribute necessary supplies for the Pause Protection Packs (or PPPs) including hot sauce and hygiene gel - their Prime Products (or PPs).
Group Leader: Elliot

GROUP B
Pause Poses
(Or PPs as well)
Special Duties:
To learn various poses like 'laughter' or 'happiness' that can be used during the Pause to trick the Terribles. (Pausewalkers are encouraged to develop their own Personal Primary Pausewalker Pause Pose (known as a PPPPP).)
Group Leader:
Buster

It was vital that every Pausewalker was trained in each. It was no good knowing your PP if you didn't know your PPP, and if you didn't know your PPP, then how could we be certain you knew your PPPP or your PPPPP?

Hamish suddenly needed a pee.

But first he walked with Alice from group to group, watching them learn. He felt pure pride (or PP).

The only kid who didn't seem to be joining in was Dexter. He sat off to one side, staring at the ground, looking a little green around the gills.

'Okay!' shouted Buster, in front of his small gathering. 'Let's say the Pause happens during a "happy" time – I want you to freeze on your best happy faces!'

All the kids made happy faces and stood perfectly Paused.

'Okay – now let's say the Pause happens during a period of subtle unrest tinged with sadness and yearning. Give me your best "subtle unrest tinged with sadness and yearning" faces!'

Next they moved to the PPPP kids learning battle techniques.

'Let's try the Mexican Foot Stamp one more time,' shouted Grenville, who was now in his element. 'And after the Mexican Foot Stamp we're going to go for the Chinese Tongue Pull! Buster tells me the Terribles have great thick wiry hair on their tongue warts – perfect for grabbing a clump of!'

As they wandered on, Hamish noticed two small figures standing in the darkness, shadowed by leaves, at the side of the clearing.

It was Scratch Tuft and Mole Stunk.

They'd been grounded for days and were holding hands. They seemed nervous to approach. After all, Hamish looked to be in charge and maybe he was still mad at them.

'Come in, girls,' he said, kindly. 'You could be handy. In fact, remember that thing you always do where one of you kneels down behind somebody and the other one pushes them over? I need you to teach us that. And also that thing you do where you break wind and then somehow catch it in your hand.'

The girls smiled, relieved. Either they were happy to be included, or they'd just broken wind again.

'Okay – remember!' shouted Alice. 'According to the graph that Mr Bodfish helped us with, the next Pause is due at 3pm today. It should last around twenty-nine minutes and twenty-nine seconds. We need to work fast. We need to work *well*. Because after today's Pause there will only be *one more* before . . .'

She paused for dramatic effect.

'. . . the *Final Event*!'

Everyone knew they had quite some arranging to do. This *had* to work.

Because, after all . . . even *your* future might very well depend on it.

28

Fairground Friday

Hamish and Alice's plan was simple.

There were two more Pauses to come.

They'd use one Pause to prepare.

And the other to *strike*.

They knew what they needed to do. They had to get all the Terribles and their WorldStopper masters in one place at one time.

And that meant they needed to get all the people of Starkley in one place at one time.

The Terribles would think they were having the luckiest day ever.

All the grown-ups? There for the taking? No more running around, slathering about? No more clickety-clacketing on uncomfortable concrete, or fiddling about with locks and windows?

They would have a field day. They would be able to take whomever they wanted. They'd be able to take *everyone*, at once, and put this awful boring town behind them – ready for the next stage.

Then they could hit London. Paris. Rome. Berlin.

They could move on to New York. Tokyo. Toronto. Moscow. Mumbai.

They would be ready for *Total World Domination*!

And because this Pause would be the longest Pause yet, they'd have all the time in the world . . .

At least – that's what they'd think . . . and if it went wrong? If the PDF had miscalculated?

Well – disaster.

'We know that at least one Terrible has to keep an eye on the town clock,' said Alice.

The PDF were sitting around the small table in the ice-cream van, pointing at the clock on a map of Starkley.

'That's why there was one on the rollercoaster last night. They think it's the only accurate clock in town. Little do they know, we've got Hamish's Explorer.'

Clover and Venk nodded. Buster patted Hamish on the back.

'If we can draw them all away from the clock and stop them seeing it, that means they'll have no idea how long it is until the Pause is over. We just have to keep them occupied for long enough and hope that our theory is right.'

Hamish made a confident face. It was important he looked confident.

'So we're going to keep everybody in one place until the Terribles arrive,' said Hamish. 'And Buster – that's when you'll attend to the clock.'

'Understood,' said Buster. 'But how are we going to get the whole town in one place?'

The Thursday 3 p.m. Pause was on and everybody had been given a job.

Every single Pausewalker needed to move fast and with great efficiency while the town and everyone else in it was at a standstill.

'Come on!' said Hamish, leading the charge into the town square. 'Let's go!'

The kids started to dash all over the place, ready to get to work.

Except one.

'What's wrong, Grenville?' asked Hamish, confused.

Grenville was staring at something nervously. Hamish followed his eye and understood immediately.

'Those boys,' he said. 'The ones that bully you.'

'Stig,' replied Grenville, quietly. 'Stig and Bash.'

Over there, outside the sweet shop, stood the much bigger boys Hamish had seen picking on Grenville that day. The expressions on their frozen faces made it look as if they'd been up to no good just as the Pause happened.

'Well,' said Hamish, wondering if he should say what he was about to say. 'You of all people know that Pauses can be used in all sorts of ways . . .'

Grenville looked at him, confused.

Meanwhile, round the corner, Scratch and Mole darted into Starkley Library, which was even quieter than usual. They tapped '1,000 Copies' into the keypad on the photocopier. Immediately, the old grey box burst into life, spilling brightly-coloured page after brightly-coloured page onto the floor.

Scratch picked one up and studied it.

TOMORROW!
FAIRGROUND FRIDAY!
FIREWORKS AND FUN!
COME AND HEAR THE IMPORTANT ANNOUNCEMENT!

STARKLEY MAY NOT BE SO BORING, AFTER ALL!

ATTENDANCE COMPULSORY.

SIGNED,

THE MAYOR.

Hopefully, the mayor would just assume he'd signed off on this and forgotten.

Outside the library, ten kids sat on their bikes and BMXs, ready to deliver the fliers all over town.

'Batch one!' screeched Grenville, who was enjoying life as a minor authority figure. 'Go, go, go!'

Inside the newsagent's on the corner, Robin and three other kids were making stickers in the sticker machine. Moments later, they were plastering them on every lapel, lamp post and frozen budgie in Starkley.

Clover and Venk snuck into Starkley FM – the very boring radio station that only ever talked about how few traffic problems there were and how they weren't expecting any tomorrow either – and changed all the presenters' scripts to read:

'And don't forget – it's Fairground Friday tomorrow night at the fairground. Get ready for that big announcement! Attendance is mandatory!'

Then they changed all the records from boring old classical stuff to high-energy European dance pop. If that didn't get people listening – nothing would!

They put up posters, they sent out invites, they blew up

balloons, they ticked 'YES I WILL ATTEND' on people's computer calendars, they changed the website of the *Starkley Post* to read:

FAIRGROUND FRIDAY WILL ROCK!

And when twenty-nine minutes and twenty-nine seconds were up and the sky flashed above them, Starkley was suddenly awash with bunting and colour.

As they stood and watched, all Hamish and Alice could hear was a rising excitement in town. Even from the adults who'd been processed into meanies.

'Fairground Friday? It's about time there was a Fairground Friday!'

'I wonder what the exciting announcement will be.'

'I heard it's that the judges changed their mind and think Starkley is the most boring town after all!'

As a car drove by, Hamish could hear its radio blaring.

'And don't forget – it's Fairground Friday tomorrow night at the fairground. Get ready for that big announcement. Here's "Dance Your Legs Off" by Laser Face . . .'

Hamish smiled.

The word was out.

'Right,' said Grenville, suddenly thundering past. 'I think I'd better run!'

Everyone looked behind him to see what he was escaping from.

Standing right there, in the middle of Starkley town square, were Stig and Bash.

And everyone was laughing at them. Old people, young people, teachers, *everyone*.

Why?

Because Grenville had used the Pause to swap all the clothes they were wearing . . . for two very, very tight and very, very stretched romper suits.

Yes. Romper suits.

He'd 'borrowed' them from the bag of a lady with a pram, along with a couple of dummies and two little nightcaps.

Stig now had a teddy under his arm and Bash had a dolly.

'**WHAT THE . . . ?!**' shouted Stig, spitting out his dummy. '**WHY ARE YOU DRESSED AS A MASSIVE BABY?**'

'**ME?**' shouted Bash, as a crowd began to gather. '**YOU'RE THE ONE DRESSED AS A MASSIVE BABY!**'

'**YOU'RE THE MASSIVE BABY!**' yelled Stig.

'NO, YOU'RE THE MASSIVE BABY!' shouted Bash.

Stig threw a rattle at Bash. Bash picked it up and threw it back.

And that was when the fight began.

'BABY FIGHT!' shouted Madame Cous Cous, bursting out of her shop and rubbing her hands with glee. 'I BLINKING *LOVE* A BABY FIGHT!'

And, as the two giant babies began to wrestle on the ground, the people of Starkley started to chant the words *'Ba-by Fight! Ba-by Fight!'*

Hamish smiled as he walked away. The plan was starting to come together; he just hoped the PDF could pull this off. So many people were relying on them, whether they knew it or not.

But now that everyone was coming to Fairground Friday, there was just one part left.

The scary part.

Which is when Dexter, the silent boy in the stripy top, ran up and tapped Hamish on the shoulder.

'I think I've got something quite important to say,' he whispered, nervously.

29

Well Done, Dexter!

'You saw their lair, Dexter?' said Hamish, shocked. 'You've *been*?'

Dexter was breathing into a paper bag to stop him hyperventilating.

'Yes,' he said, quietly, between great gulps of air.

'Show us where it is,' said Alice. 'On this map.'

Dexter pointed the finger of one shaking hand to a part of the woods somewhere north of the grey bridge.

'Over the bridge?' asked Hamish. 'But no one goes there.'

'Scared?' said Alice.

'Well . . . yes,' admitted Hamish. 'Aren't you?'

'I told you,' she said. 'I'm scared of nothing.'

'You seemed a bit scared up that rollercoaster,' said Venk.

'Shuddup, Venk!' said Alice. 'Or I'll tell everyone you want to be in a boyband!'

'There's an old stone cottage,' continued Dexter, doing his best not to stutter with fear. 'Down by the cliffs.'

The cliffs? It was dangerous down by the cliffs. The cliffs were all that separated Starkley from the sea.

'It's almost green with moss,' said Dexter, 'but the leaves in the trees around it are all black, like tar, like they've been poisoned.'

'How did you find it?' asked Alice.

'We were going for a walk two weeks ago,' said Dexter, shivering at the memory. 'Me and my parents and my older sister. Dad said it seemed to be getting darker and then there was this flash, and suddenly my whole family just stopped walking.'

'Except you?'

'Except me,' said Dexter. 'And then I heard them approaching. It sounded like drums or thunder and I didn't know what to do, so I hid behind a bush . . .'

Hamish put his hand on Dexter's shoulder. It was trembling.

'They came from everywhere. Left, right, up, down. They scooped my family up, and after a minute or so I got up and followed all the broken branches and bushes to the creepy old cottage . . .'

'So they live in a cottage?' said Buster, wrinkling his nose. 'What – like a *grandma*? Full of doilies and knitting?'

'They live *under* the cottage,' said Dexter, his face almost grey at the memory. 'You open the front door and there's nothing but stairs going down. You can see the first one or two, but then it's just darkness . . . blacker than you can imagine.'

'Did you go down?' asked Alice, moving closer. 'Did you walk down the stairs?'

Dexter looked ashamed.

'I managed the first step. But I knew what was down there. I'd seen them. And what's worse – I'd seen who was in charge.'

'The WorldStoppers?' said Hamish. 'The big ones with the moustaches?'

'Bigger even than them,' said Dexter. 'Taller than a bus. Taller than two buses, maybe. He had the biggest hands in the world. They were like claws. And his legs were like trees. I can still hear the sound of him walking, Hamish. This stomp . . . stomp . . . *STOMP.*'

The kids all jumped slightly.

'I think I saw the WorldStopper General,' he said, eyes wide and fearful.

Alice gulped. There was something even worse than a WorldStopper? There was a WorldStopper *General*?

Hamish knew what this meant. The boss was in town to make sure the job got done. That was not good news. But at least now they knew who must be in charge of the Pauses.

'I couldn't go any further,' said Dexter, still quite shaken. 'I was too scared.'

He hung his head in shame.

Hamish patted Dexter on the back and then looked at Alice.

'Underneath that cottage is where we'll find our families,' he said.

Now there was just the small matter of the WorldStoppers themselves.

The Final Countdown

On that fateful Friday morning, feeling he'd prepared as much as was humanly possible, Hamish Ellerby closed the door of 13 Lovelock Close for what he hoped would not be the last time ever.

One more Pause, he thought. *One more Pause in which to change* everything.

'**SHADDUP!**' he heard, as he clicked the door closed behind him. '**YOU LITTLE PIPSCRIMPERS! I'LL WALLOP YOUR LOLLOPS!**'

In the garden next door, Mr Ramsface had a cruel and twisted look across his chops. He was chasing his children around the garden with a hosepipe, which was furiously spurting ice-cold water all over the place.

But this was not a fun game. The children were soaked already and running around in circles, confused.

'Dad!' they were shouting, unaware their father had been processed by the WorldStoppers. 'Stop it!'

'YOU LITTLE SMERKS!' he yelled.

Behind him, Mrs Ramsface appeared. Hamish was relieved. She'd stop him. She'd talk some sense into him.

But she didn't.

Instead, she started pelting the kids with tennis balls and bags of flour.

'YOU WABBLING LITTLE RETCH-BEANS!' she shouted. **'YOU NASTY OLD DINGLES!'**

'Mummy!' shouted little Billy Ramsface. 'For the love of Giant Squid, *stoppit*!'

There was a tense atmosphere in town too.

Madame Cous Cous was putting up a sign outside her International World of Treats and barking at it.

THIS SHOP NO LONGER SERVES:
CHILDREN · FRIENDS OF CHILDREN
GROWN-UPS · ANIMALS (especially CHICKENS)
GROWN-UPS DRESSED AS ANIMALS
(especially CHICKENS)
FRIENDS OF GROWN-UPS DRESSED AS ANIMALS
(especially CHICKENS)

As Hamish rounded a corner, he watched in quiet astonishment as Rex Ox wrestled with Tyrus Quinn on a street corner.

Children cowered in Shop Til You Pop, their faces pressed up against the glass, wondering what on earth was going on outside.

By the newsagent, the poster for the *Starkley Post* read:

OFFICIAL:
EVERYTHING IS RUBBISH.

Over to one side, the Postmaster had set her post office trolley on fire and was pointing at it, laughing maniacally. She'd left a trail of opened presents behind her on the street, which mingled with torn-down flyers for Fairground Friday.

Frau Fussbundler appeared to have given up going to school as well and was outside the butcher's arm-wrestling with Mr Longblather, who was dressed as a furious chicken (though no one quite knew why).

And everywhere – *everywhere* – was the sound of meanness.

Getting louder, swirling through the air like a whirlwind, picking up anger and spreading it across the town.

Things were reaching crisis point.

'In less than twenty-four hours, the Final Event is due,' said Alice, addressing the Pausewalkers. 'We have one Pause left to stop it ever happening. It's our last chance to bring our families back.'

The kids were all sitting around the ice-cream van, the flashing blue light reflected in their eyes.

Hamish felt an incredible surge of warmth towards Alice. Throughout all this, she'd always been there for him. Like a guardian. And he, he hoped, had always been there for her. They were a good team. Everyone had a lot to be proud of.

'You should all have received a temporary tattoo by now.'

Hamish looked at his own arm. It read: **UP! United Pausewalkers!**

'This is so you can immediately recognise another Pausewalker,' she said. 'Because tonight things could get messy. At around half past eight – at sunset – there will be a Pause. When that happens, Buster will stop the town clock.'

Buster raised his hand.

'But if literally everyone is at the fair and I'm all alone in the middle of town, how will I know if the world has stopped? I mean – it'll just be me. All on my own. With nothing to look at to see if it's stopped!'

Alice realised Buster had made an excellent point. That may well have been the first time ever.

'We'll turn on the light at the top of the rollercoaster,' she said, thinking quickly. 'You'll be able to see that from where you are and then you'll know for certain that the world has stopped. The rest of you – when the Terribles arrive, do not scream. Do not run. Do not even move. Do nothing at all, until Hamish gives you the signal. And then – *cause as much chaos as possible*!'

Hamish looked out at the kids in front of him. They seemed scared.

Hamish realised he was too.

But he also knew one thing: he was going to get his family back.

At 8 p.m. as the light began to fade, the children started to make their way to the fairground.

A huge crowd of Starkley residents was already heading towards it. The Processed mixed with the remaining

Normals, making for an unusual atmosphere.

'Outta my way,' a Processed would say.

'Oh, I'm terribly sorry,' a Normal would reply.

'Shuddup, beanbag face,' a Processed might reply.

'Well, there's no need for that,' the Normal would say back.

'Well, there's no need for YOU!' the Processed would snap.

Hamish stood by the rollercoaster and kept his eye on everybody as they walked in. He guessed that maybe ninety per cent of the grown-ups had now been processed. Tonight would be the night the Terribles would want to finish the job.

As they entered the fairground and smelled the popcorn and petrol and acres of candyfloss, the kids all spread out as agreed. They plastered on fake smiles and laughed out loud so that anyone might think they were just normal children, enjoying the fair, rather than members of a highly-organised and elite Pause resistance unit.

Hamish kept his eye on The Explorer. Someone turned up the music as light became dark.

'8.25,' he whispered to Alice. 'Five minutes to go.'

More and more grown-ups arrived and walked through the big brass gates to the fair. Soon they were jumping on the rides and bickering over who was first in the queue.

Grown men shouted at each other as they purposefully tried to crash the dodgems into one another. Women threw balls at a coconut shy with all the ferocity of a Wimbledon tennis star serving a record-breaking shot.

'8.28,' whispered Alice, and Hamish cast a look around the fairground to make sure everybody was in position.

'Right,' she said. 'I'm going to test the rollercoaster light so that Buster knows when to stop the clock.'

She moved to the small control room by the side of the rollercoaster and flicked the switch.

'Did that work?' she said, looking up.

'Try it again,' said Hamish.

She flipped the switch.

But the little red light at the top of the rollercoaster stayed dark.

'It's broken!' she said, flipping it again, up and down and up and down and up again. 'It must have got knocked by that Terrible the other night!'

She put her hands to her mouth in horror.

'The light! The signal! What time is it?'

Hamish checked his watch.

'8.29!' he said, panicking.

'If Buster doesn't see the signal and stop the town clock

275

then this whole thing is wasted! The Terribles will come and just grab everyone and they'll be able to see how much time they have left and take them all. What do we do? What do we do?'

Hamish's mind raced.

This couldn't all be for nothing. This final chance, this last attack!

He spun around.

'There! Look!' he said.

He pointed at a tent marked **FIREWORKS**. They were supposed to be for the big midnight finish.

'Come on!'

Hamish and Alice raced to the tent and pulled out every single firework they could. Big ones, small ones, enormous ones, ones shaped like candles, ones shaped like rockets, ones with little spinny windmills on the front.

'We need to set them off,' said Hamish. 'We need to set them *all* off!'

With incredible speed, Hamish and Alice started sticking them in the ground.

'We're not supposed to be touching these!' she said. 'We're ten!'

'We're not exactly supposed to be Earth's only defence against dreadful rampaging monsters either!' said Hamish. 'Now quickly – we only have about thirty seconds until the Pause!'

'WHAT ARE YOU DOING?' yelled a man, striding towards them. **'GET AWAY FROM THOSE!'**

'There!' shouted Alice. 'That's all of them!'

'A match! We need a match! Where are we going to get a match?!'

Wait!

Hamish felt in his back pocket and pulled out a small box.

BELASKO.

Of course! The matchbox from his dad's desk!

He poured out the sunflower seeds he'd put there days earlier and found a match.

'YOU STOP RIGHT THERE!' screamed the man.

Quickly, Hamish struck it against the box and held it out in front of him.

As the first firework began to fizz, he lit the next. And the next. And the next.

'I'M GOING TO GET YOUR MUM AND DAD!' shouted the man.

No, thought Hamish. I *am*.

And, as the first firework fizzed and popped and pirouetted into the air, Hamish kept going, lighting and lighting and lighting, until waaaaaaay up in the air, the first firework EXPLODED, lighting up the night sky . . .

Another firework **BOOMED** as three more whizzed off into the air . . .

Then another . . .

Then six more . . .

BOOM! BANG! BOOM! BOOM!

FLASH!

And all was still.

The Pause had begun.

Hamish and Alice looked up into the night sky.

Six huge, stunning, colourful explosions hung still in the air.

Trails of what looked like falling stardust frozen in the blackness, illuminating the ground below, as perfectly Paused grown-ups stared up at their sparkling, glistening wonder.

'It's beautiful,' said Alice, watching them sparkle, and, for a second, they could have been anywhere at all.

A perfect silence stretched right the way across Starkley.

No one moved.

And then each and every Pausewalker stiffened as the quiet thunder began.

'Assume your positions!' yelled Hamish and the PDF sprang into action.

The Terribles were coming. And they were coming fast.

Showdown

'Has everyone done it?' yelled Alice. 'Has everyone changed a watch?'

'I've changed four!' shouted Grenville.

'I've changed six!' said Venk.

'PPPs are distributed!' yelled Elliot.

'Which ones are PPPs again?' asked Clover, confused. 'Are they like the PPPs or more like the PPPs?'

The thunder of hooves was getting louder and louder and LOUDER.

Alice looked up at the sky full of fireworks.

'I hope Buster realises,' she said, almost under her breath.

'Buster is smart,' said Hamish, reassuring her. 'Buster will realise we had to change plans. He'll see that the fireworks have stopped in mid-air. He'll work out that the Pause has started. I *guarantee* it!'

M

Across town, by the clock, Buster was staring up at the little light on the rollercoaster and scrunching up his nose.

That was weird. Why wasn't it on?

It should be on by now, he thought.

He looked up at the clock. Yes. That little red light should definitely be on by now.

Buster yawned.

Oh, he thought, absent-mindedly. *Look at the pretty fireworks.*

ℍ

'They're nearly here!' shouted Hamish, as the noise of the approaching horde grew. 'Adopt your PPs!'

'What are our PPs again?' whispered Clover. 'Our Pretty Pickles? Our Picnic Pimples?'

'Your Pause Pose!' said Venk. 'Do your Pause Pose!'

And as Venk froze like a statue, staring up at the fireworks and grinning an enormous, joyful grin . . . the smell wafted into them, around them, *through* them.

That putrid, rancid, unbearable stench, like a cloud of foul and rotten damp. Each and every Pausewalker noticed their nostrils flare as it hit them. Some held their breath. Others breathed it in and felt their eyes well up.

The thundering had stopped.

You might think that was a good thing.

But that was *not* a good thing.

That meant they were here. Creeping in from the shadows, sneaking in and taking stock . . .

Hamish felt one before he saw one.

It was behind him, trailing one bony finger from the small of his back to the nape of his neck, its nail just strong enough to break a little of his skin.

He could feel he wanted to shiver.

But he mustn't.

He mustn't.

The Terrible moved around him now, until it was facing him.

It towered above him and, as it began to move its face down towards his, Hamish could sense dozens more moving into the fairground.

Finally, the beast was at eye level.

His heart lurched as Hamish twigged something . . . He *recognised* it.

It was the very same Terrible that had been at his window that night.

And the Terrible obviously recognised him too. That was why it had tried to make him shiver. It wanted to *prove* that Hamish *was* a Pausewalker.

It raised one finger into the air, then did the most awful thing it possibly could.

It started to slowly slide it into Hamish's nostril . . .

W

Back at the clock, Buster definitely thought something was wrong.

That little red light had not come on. It was just sitting there, doing nothing, high up on that rollercoaster, under all those pretty fireworks.

Those fireworks that were just hanging there.

Like fireworks do.

Buster yawned again. *Man, The Beast needs feeding*, he thought, tapping his tummy.

Wait – *fireworks? Hanging?*

That's not what fireworks do!

Oh, dear.

Oh, dear me.

It's the last Pause!

Buster scrambled for the clock.

W

Hamish counted all the ways that this was absolutely, definitely the most disgusting thing that had ever happened to him as the Terrible's finger slithered out of one nostril

283

and started to slide painfully up the other.

There were about a thousand ways that this was absolutely, definitely the most disgusting thing that had ever happened to him.

He could feel that cold, smooth finger now behind his eyes, feeling for his brain.

And yet, somehow, Hamish remained absolutely still.

Still, because he *had* to.

For Mum.

For Jimmy.

For Starkley.

For his *dad*.

The Terrible cocked its head and moved its dreadful face closer to his. Hamish could see his own reflection in its

enormous bug eyes, the way you might see your own when you look into an old scratched spoon.

He could also see Alice, off to one side, lit by the fireworks, and not moving a muscle.

Other Terribles were having the time of their lives. They were playing catch with some grown-ups, tossing them back and forth, while another used a cat as a hat and giggled.

By the dodgems, poor Robin had to stand completely still while one particular Terrible began to drape worms across his head, like a sort of worm-wig. Robin's eyes were as wide as they could get – because *worms*! – but that boy did not move. Even when the Terrible began to squish the worms down and rub them in, all the while smiling a Terrible smile. Robin could feel their wet little bodies slippering and slathering around on his skull. He had to fight with everything inside him not to whimper and flee.

Come on, thought Hamish, desperate to get on with this, desperate to stop these things from treating his friend that way. *Come on!*

And then . . .

STOMP. . . STOMP. . . STOMP. . .

This was it.

The WorldStoppers were arriving.

But Hamish was not prepared for this.

Two giant WorldStoppers strode into the fairground and began to laugh a deep, guttural, spine-jangling laugh . . .

They looked at the entire population of Starkley, together in one place, and they could not believe their luck. They clapped their hands together, palm juice splittering and splattering everywhere, and they cried out in glee.

And a moment later, perhaps summoned by the joy . . .

STOMP.
STOMP.
STOMP.

The Terribles turned to face the noise. Some of them kneeled to welcome it.

Hamish quickly looked at Dexter, who looked back at him and nodded, scared.

The WorldStopper General was coming.

Two enormous trees bent sideways as a beast the size of *three* buses crashed its way into the fair. Its huge hands were the size of cars and it flung an entire Super Swinging Viking Boat out of its way to make room. A throng of angry,

wet Requines galloped in behind it and circled the frozen people of Starkley. They stood, sinister and muscular, and whinnied.

'**GOOOOOOD**,'

it roared, the noise vibrating through the town.

'**THESE CHILLENS BE GIVING ME A MINDGRAIN. YOU GEDDUM.**'

Hamish's heart was in his mouth. He had never – ever – imagined the WorldStopper General to be so . . . grenormous!

So . . . enormassive!

So . . . big.

Vast glumps of spittle flew through the air, whistling past the kids and splattering on the rides and stopped-still grown-ups.

'ALL OV THE CHILLENS! AND YOU GEDDUM!'

Whatever it had said, it was clear that the Terribles were about to obey.

Hamish looked at Alice. She winked at him.

'PAUSEWALKERS!' he shouted. 'NOW!'

32

This is It!

The very instant he'd realised his error, Buster had clambered up the town clock and stuck a spanner on the clock face to stop the minute hand from moving any further.

There. That should do it. And he knew precisely what to do next.

He slid down again and jumped through the door of the ice-cream van.

He'd made a few modifications he was certain might come in handy.

At the fairground, all was complete and utter insanity.

It was *chaos*!

Children were running everywhere, some of them banging spoons on tins and saucepans, while confused Terribles spun around, trying to catch them and bumping into one another.

'GEDDUM!' yelled the

WorldStopper General, furious at this distraction.

'CRUSHEM!
CRACKEM!'

Hamish kept one eye on the crazed and flailing giant.
It seemed panicky.

'HOOS CHECKIN
THA TIME?' it roared.
'HOOS WATCHIN
THA CLOCK?' i

At the bottom of the rollercoaster, three Terribles tried
desperately to scramble over one another, doing whatever
they could to climb up the poles at the bottom. They
couldn't understand why they kept sliding down.

Quickly, Venk splurted out even more of the super-slippy hygiene gel that was keeping the poles so slidey.

'WE NEEDS TO SEE THA CLOCK!'

shouted the WorldStopper General.

'GRAB DOZE WEANS AN' STOPPEM!'

But the Terribles were no longer listening to their master. They had other things to deal with.

'MEXICAN FOOT STAMP!' screamed Grenville, in his element, as a bunch of kids stamped on a Terrible's foot. **'CHINESE TONGUE-PULL THAT RIDICULOUS BEAST!'**

Through the middle of them, Elliot ran, squirting hot sauce from his dad's old aftershave bottle as Terribles spluttered and pawed at their eyes.

'WHATSA TIME?'

roared the WorldStopper General, his exasperated spit now landing in huge great puddle-clumps on the ground.

BOOM! Down came one of his feet!
BOOM! Down came the other!

One Terrible had now made it to the very top of the rollercoaster and was peering out at the town clock. But it hadn't changed! It was just the same as it was when they started! Confused and confounded, it shrugged its angular shoulders and made a pained face at its boss.

'CHECK THA FROZEN'S WATCHES THEN!'

yelled the WorldStopper General.

'WE GUESS HOW LONGS WE GOT!'

But every watch on every person showed a very different time.

4.13!

9.29!

17.37!

'WE'S GONNA RETREATS!'

shouted the WorldStopper General, panicked and realising he was in no way prepared for this kind of organised revolution.

'WE'S GOTTA RETREATS!'

Hamish checked The Explorer. The only watch that showed the *true* time! He had to time this *just* right . . .

He waited . . .

He waited a moment more . . .

Then . . .

'Now, Clover!' shouted Hamish. 'Go!'

And, as a Terrible brought out the Bugle to sound the Screech of Retreat, Clover flung off the incredibly realistic bright green bush costume she'd been hiding in all along. . .

. . . aaaand . . .

GRABBED IT!

'Alice!' she shouted. 'Catch!'

To the WorldStopper General's horror, Clover threw it up, up, up in the air . . .

. . .The Bugle spun, and pirouetted, and slapped straight into Alice's hand like she was catching a boomerang. She stared at it, stunned, for a second.

'Go!' shouted Hamish, tapping his watch. 'RUN!'

But Alice did not move. It was like she was frozen.

'NOW, ALICE!' shouted Hamish again. 'GO!'

But still she just stared at the Bugle.

And now the WorldStopper General, seeing exactly what was about to happen, began to stomp towards her . . . She looked up to see him approaching . . .

Which is when Robin jumped in front of the WorldStopper General and began to wave his arms.

Hang on – *Robin*?

'It's 12.03!' shouted Starkley's once-most-nervous kid. 'It's 9.15! It's half past June! It's seventy minutes to yesterday!'

It was enough to confuse the great beast for a second. What was this small boy banging on about? This child who stank of worms?

He's buying time! thought Hamish. *Which is exacly what the WorldStoppers are running out of!*

Alice snapped out of it. Her face flipped from confusion to determination. She could *do* this.

And, as the WorldStopper General lost patience and swatted Robin away and into the bouncy castle, Alice Shepherd ran like her life depended on it, which, to be honest, it did.

She ran with amazing speed and dexterity.

She ran between legs and jumped over long arms that tried to grab and slap her to the ground.

She leapt over spit-puddles and slid through the mud, and, as she reached the end of the fairground, the Starkley Under-12s 100-metre champion did everything she could to escape the clutches of the fearsome, furious WorldStopper General, now crashing and roaring behind her.

Next to a sign marked:

FARMER JARMER'S PRIVATE PROPERTY

she slid to a halt.

Hamish had told her his hunch. He'd better be right about this.

And just when WorldStopper General's enormous, grasping hands were so *almost* upon her, Alice Shepherd heaved that great shell-like Bugle right into the vast and swaying field of sunflowers at the fairground's edge . . .

'NOOOOOOOO!'

bellowed the WorldStopper General.

'THE BUGLE! ISS AMONGST THE FUNSLOWERS! RETREATS! RETREATS!'

FLASH!

BOOM! BOOM! BOOM! BOOM! BOOM! BOOM! BOOM!

Fireworks! Explosions overhead!

Hamish stood alone, lit by flashes of green and red and blue, smiling at his Explorer. They'd done it. The Pause was over. The noise and colour picked up exactly where it left off, with the kind of huge, full explosions you could feel right there in your chest.

The brilliant flashes from above were like strobe lights, capturing split seconds of life, like a camera flash. On the ground, you just couldn't tell who was still and who was moving.

Hamish looked around him cautiously. The people of Starkley all stared up at the sky as the fireworks reached their powerful finale . . . The Terribles seemed still too . . . but were they?

And, as the final **BOOM!** echoed and bounced around the buildings of Starkley, there was a smattering of appreciative applause as thick smoke drifted across the fair.

And then there was nothing.

But, as the smoke began to clear, the screams began.

'What the heck are THEY?' yelled one man, tripping over himself as he ran.

'MONSTERS!' screamed another.

'Look at the size of it!' shrieked a woman, pointing at the WorldStopper General, who towered over the town, blank-eyed and unmoving.

'Oh my goodness!' screamed Mr Ramsface, the spell of meanness now apparently broken. 'Oh my goodness!'

The screaming continued as the grown-ups began to run from the fair, every now and again slapping into another stopped, slimy Terrible and screaming louder still. The screams of terror were soon joined by the mighty cheers of the Pausewalkers.

They had stopped them. They had stopped the stoppers. They were the StopperStoppers!

Hamish looked at Alice triumphantly.

'They're frozen!' he said, poking one finger up a Terrible's jelly-like nostril.

There was now just one thing left to do.

33

The One Thing
Left To Do

The plinkety-plonk of the National Anthem was the next thing anybody heard as Buster motored the ice-cream van through the fairground and skidded to a halt in the mud. The music was louder this time though. Buster had clearly added some serious bass.

'Why's it so muddy?' he said, from the window. 'It hasn't been raining, has it?'

'*That* thing!' said Hamish, pointing at the WorldStopper General, still towering above them, frozen in time. 'He spits when he talks!'

'I called the army like you told me to,' said Buster. 'Spoke to a very nice lady on reception called Sandra. She said she'd pass the details on.'

'What have you done to the van?' said Alice, surprised. It certainly looked different. Buster had changed the tyres to the type you'd normally see on a tractor. It looked like one of those monster trucks you get in America. It was ginormous!

'Just a little modification for Stage 2 of the plan,' he said, proudly, and far higher up than he'd ever sat before. 'Do you like the new respray? I thought black and gold gave it a certain important look.'

'Pausewalkers!' shouted Hamish, as Buster set a gigantic blue light flashing. 'On your bikes!'

The van sped through the woods now, rumbling over the bumps and lumps and making light work of them. Behind it, a dozen Pausewalkers rode their gleaming Vespas, lights cutting brightly through the night.

Inside the Battle Van, Hamish thought of his poor family. This had to work. Alice studied the map with Dexter.

'We have to head for the cliffs,' he said, pointing up ahead, and frowning at the memory of it. 'We have to go over the bridge . . .'

One after another, the team shot over Starkley's little grey bridge, leaving the safety of town behind. That little bridge reminded Hamish of the last time he'd thought of it. When was that again?

'Of course,' said Hamish, remembering that day at Grenville's. 'There was a map at the Postmaster's. It was marked **ROUTES** with all the arrows pouring out of the woods. I thought it was for postmen. But it was for Terribles! It makes sense – the Postmaster knows Starkley better than anyone and they got to her first! She was first to be taken! Her map helped them plan their raids. It told them precisely where everyone lived!'

'That must be why they always came at night at first,' said Alice. 'Because they knew people would be in bed!'

Excitement and fear hung heavy in the air as they passed a sign marked **THE CLIFFS**.

'We're nearly there,' said Dexter, with fear in his eyes. 'We have to go by foot from here.'

'*Then by foot we will go*,' said Hamish, determined.

Waves crashed against the foot of the cliffs as Hamish hopped out of the van.

The air up here was wet with the spitter and spatter of the sea. An unforgiving wind whipped around the gang.

'So this is it,' said Hamish, heroically, spying the cottage in the distance.

'What?' said Clover, over the roar of the sea.

'I said "so this is it",' said Hamish, a bit less heroically this time.

'Can you SPEAK UP?' shouted Clover. 'Only it's *really LOUD* here.'

Hamish's hair was damp now and he wiped it from his eyes. The cottage looked small from here, lit by one old and orange gas lamp hanging at the door, squeaking as it swung in the wind.

'Hamish . . .' said Buster, close to Hamish's ear, and Hamish turned to face him. 'I hope you find your dad.'

Hamish saw the sadness in Buster's eyes.

'Thank you, Buster,' he said. Then, 'You know, I think your dad would have been so proud of you tonight.'

Buster smiled.

'Really?'

'Yes,' said Hamish. 'If we've saved the world – and who knows if we have yet – then a large part of that is down to you. Plus, look what you did to the van. I think if he's watching somewhere, he'll be telling everybody . . . "that kid there . . . that's my son".'

Buster smiled, then had to look away. He nodded to himself and smiled some more.

'It's time,' said Alice, as the crash of an angry wave rose high into the air.

The old stone cottage was just as creepy as Dexter had described.

Well, actually, it turned out Dexter wasn't very good at descriptions, because it was far, far creepier.

The entire building seemed damp. Not from the sea, but like there was an invisible river running down its front, keeping it permanently moist.

'Secure the area!' yelled Hamish. 'Clover – make sure the whole place is surrounded! Venk – take some Pausewalkers and make sure help is coming!'

Hamish studied the cottage. Its door was made of ancient, splintered wood, with an old black knocker in the middle like a snarling dragon. Gargoyles hung from either side of the roof. And there were flies and egg-sized black bees *everywhere*.

Who knew what was in there?

Bravely, Hamish pulled open the door.

He blinked.

He saw absolutely nothing inside.

Just blackness.

Beside him, Alice trembled.

'I know I said I wasn't scared of anything,' she said, taking his hand. 'But there is one thing.'

'The dark?' said Hamish. 'You don't have to come with me.'

Then Hamish remembered the little keyring with the torch attachment he'd packed in his original PSK. He knew that would come in handy! He turned it on and held it out in front of him. But this blackness was too black. It was powerfully black. It was like the light from his little torch was just sucked away into the void. He was going to need a lot more power than this.

'Let me give that a little boost,' said Buster, smiling.

Five minutes later, the van and every Vespa they had were shining their headlights into the nothingness, on full-beam.

Now Hamish could make out the first few steps . . .

And so, nodding at Alice and taking one deep breath, Hamish stepped inside.

The Depths

Down, down, deeper and deeper inched Hamish, holding his tiny torch in front of him.

With every pitch-black step, he expected to reach the bottom.

But this was not a basement. These steps seemed endless.

He could sense there were no walls either side of him now. Just the steps. The steps that seemed to be getting narrower and narrower and narrower, until he could only move forward by putting one foot directly in front of the other.

'Are you still there?' he asked, nervously.

'I'm still with you,' said Alice, putting one slightly shaking hand on his shoulder. 'I'm not going to leave you. We're in this together.'

So on and on they went, secretly dreading they might hear a creak, or a shriek, or anything from the depths that might indicate a leftover Terrible was slinking or skittering about.

Where would this lead them, this black nothingness? Was this one step too far? The stupidest thing they'd ever do? A trap?

'Wait!' said Hamish, finally. 'I think I'm at the bottom!'

He tapped his foot. The floor had changed. It was harder. Tiny pebbles and chipped stone crunched and gristled underfoot. Hamish's torch began to flicker and struggle in the soul-sucking blackness.

'Try the matches again,' said Alice. *'Please.'*

Hamish struck one and, as it fizzed to life, he thought he could make out something of interest, a few metres away. The light of the match grew feeble, so he lit another, moved a few centimetres forward, then lit one more.

The air was thicker down here. It felt as if he could feel the dank moss tickle his throat as he breathed it in. It was cold too and both Hamish and Alice could watch misty plumes of their breath rise in the brief glow of each dying match.

It was almost perfectly silent, save for a few distant clanks and clunks, like old radiators in the dead of night . . .

Hamish could now sense something directly in front of him.

He reached out to touch it.

It was cold.

Wet.

Slimy.

Right there, barely an arm's length away, was a vast iron door.

Hamish felt for the lock.

It still had the key in.

ᛗ

Down the corridor they walked.

There was more light here – an ancient brass gas lamp hung at the end of the passageway, casting long shadows across the stones of the wall.

Their footsteps sounded so small in this place.

'It's so cold,' whispered Alice.

'Wait,' said Hamish, his arm out in front of him. 'Look . . .'

At the dimmest end of the horrible underground corridor was another door – this one arched and scratched and scuffed.

There was no handle – just a small round hole at the top. . .

'There must be a handle on the inside,' said Hamish. 'We're going to have to reach inside and find it to open the door . . .'

Alice shook her head.

'No,' she said. 'Who knows what's inside that hole? There could be more Terribles. Or maybe it's where they keep their Requines! Or maybe there's a spider monster, or a giant rat, or the suckers of a fifteen-metre octopus, or just a massive wet tongue! Let's get the others. We can't do this alone.'

'We're here now,' said Hamish. 'It's just us. You and me. It's up to us.'

If he could have seen Alice properly in this darkness, he would have seen the palest, most sick-looking girl in Starkley.

But then she shut her eyes and squeezed her arms around herself.

'Fine,' she said, firmly. 'Let's do it.'

From somewhere on the other side of the door, they could suddenly hear whispers. Movement. The hair on the back of Hamish's neck stood up. Alice felt goosebumps rise all the way up her arms and shoulders and she shivered.

'I'm going for it,' said Hamish, and slowly he slid one arm into the hole, breaking a thin film of slime and feeling it pop like a bubble and run down his wrist.

He shut his eyes tight.

Please don't be a spider monster. Please don't be a massive tongue.

Alice could hear more shuffling from behind that door now. She could hear breaths and footsteps and clanks and bangs, and –

'Hurry, Hamish!' she said, not wanting to think what might be about to grab onto his poor arm. 'I don't like this!'

'Got it,' said Hamish, clunking something down and feeling the door frame release its door with a musty *voof*.

Hamish and Alice reached out to hold one another's hands, as the door creaked open in front of them . . .

And as they stood there, petrified, they sensed movement from inside.

'Come on,' said Hamish, trembling, and putting one foot into the darkness . . .

From somewhere down to their right, behind five thick iron bars, lit by a small flame on the wall . . .

A woman stood.

A *human*.

'Mum!' cried Alice, pressing herself up against the bars.

'Alice?' said the lady. 'Oh, Alice! We've been so worried! Stephen – it's Alice!'

'Run!' said a man next to Alice's mum. 'Get out of here, Alice!'

There were more voices now. Voices everywhere.

'It's okay, Dad!' said Alice, now crying tears of relief, and sliding out the rusty metal bar that held their door closed. 'I'm with Hamish Ellerby!'

Something was set off inside Hamish.

Some kind of excitement, some kind of euphoria.

Dad! he thought.

He began to run down the corridor, opening cage after cage, peering in, moving to the next one.

There was old Mr Picklelips!

Dexter's whole family!

There was Felicity Gobb!

There was the bloke who ran the gym! Wow – no one had even noticed that guy had gone!

On and on down the vast, dank corridor Hamish pounded, searching for his family, searching for his *dad*, until . . .

'Hamish!'

He spun round.

'Mum!' he said. 'Jimmy!'

'Oh, Hamish!' she said, reaching out for him.

'It's James?' said Jimmy. 'Have you seen Felicity?'

'Where's Dad?' said Hamish, grabbing his mum's hands. 'Where's my dad?'

Her face fell.

'Oh, Hamish,' she said.

'What?' he said. 'He's here, right? Of course he's here! He has to be here!'

'Oh, my baby boy,' she said again, and even in the gloom Hamish could see her eyes were filled with tears.

'Don't you tell me he's not here,' said Hamish, falling to his knees. '*Please*, Mum! Don't you tell me that after all this, my dad is not here . . .'

ᚻᚻ

Outside the stone cottage, the Pausewalkers cheered every new grown-up who appeared through the door, blinking as they shielded their eyes from the headlights.

Families embraced. Children were hoisted high into the air and cuddled and squeezed and breathed in.

Above them all, army helicopters now circled the woods, shining vast, broad beams of white light beneath them.

Frozen Terribles were being caged up and flown away on winches, into the ink-black sky, over the thundering sea.

'Hamish,' said Buster, with the hugest smile, and holding a lady's hand, tightly. 'This is my mum!'

Hamish tried his best to smile and said 'Hello' as brightly as he could.

Felicity and Jimmy were having an argument about why

she never Skyped him back. Apparently Jimmy didn't think being kidnapped by monsters was an acceptable excuse for such mind games in their relationship.

'So your dad wasn't taken, huh?' said Alice, suddenly there.

Hamish looked at the ground and shook his head.

'Guess not,' he said.

'So he just went?' she said. 'Well, that sucks.'

'Yes, I suppose it does, yes,' said Hamish, rubbing his eyes. They were red and sore.

She smiled at him.

'You still saved Starkley, Hamish,' she said, squeezing his shoulder. 'You still saved the world.'

And, as the police sirens approached through the woods and as another Terrible was winched high into the night to be disposed of at Her Majesty's discretion, Hamish Ellerby wiped away a tear and took a breath.

'Yes,' he said, trying to nod convincingly. 'I suppose that's something.'

One Week Later

One week later, in the town square, underneath the big clock that now always seemed to run on time, Alice Shepherd beamed the biggest smile of her life.

'And this is for you,' said the mayor, leaning down to pin a medal on her top, as the whole town began to applaud. 'With our never-ending thanks.'

If it was possible, her smile grew wider still, and she waved at her parents in the audience.

It had been a great day so far. The mayor had announced that after careful consideration by the relevant judges (who had taken into account both the monster invasion and the subsequent juvenile rebellion) Starkley had officially been named Britain's *Least* Most Boring Town!

They were getting an award!

Buster had already had his medal for incredible bravery. So had Venk and Clover and Elliot, and all their parents went crazy as their names were read out. Robin literally could not believe he'd finally been called brave and his mum looked on beaming with pride as she munched on a fresh bag of Japanese Jellied Fish-Shavings. Every kid in Starkley who'd had a filling and fought the Terribles was included. Each one seemed so full of life, and colour, and excitement, as they sat on that little stage underneath a banner that read:

THANK YOU, PAUSEWALKERS!

with their silver medals on sky-blue ribbons.

Only Hamish Ellerby seemed a little out of place.

He seemed . . . grey. Like he'd forgotten how to smile. Like there was a small black cloud constantly hovering above his head.

'Come on, buddy,' whispered Grenville, who was dressed to the nines in a full-length black El Gamba costume with ceremonial cape. 'You should be happy!'

'And finally,' said the mayor, now reaching Hamish, 'Starkley would like to thank *you*, Master Hamish Ellerby of thirteen Lovelock Close . . .'

An enormous cheer went up as a brass band began to play. Tiny children all over Starkley pulled party poppers. A smiling Rex Ox used his leaf blower to thrust ticker tape high up into the air.

Hamish's mum kept tapping people's elbows and saying, 'That's my son up there – that's my Hamish!' Even Jimmy stood and applauded and whistled, proud as punch that he had such an amazing little brother.

But Hamish could not help but notice that there was still a chair next to them that was not filled.

And Hamish did not smile.

'Maybe your dad will read about it in the paper, Hamish,' said Alice, kindly, as the two friends moved away from the party. 'Maybe he'll see what he's been missing. Or maybe he'll just stay away and that'll be for the best.'

They looked out over Starkley. It was *covered* in sunflowers. Farmer Jarmer had donated a flower to every house in Starkley and each and every resident had been scattering seeds across town too. Perhaps it was an allergy, or maybe it was the size of them, but for whatever reason the Terribles hated sunflowers. Even though they'd captured all the beasts frozen in the Pause, Starkley was taking no chances.

The Bugle that Alice had thrown in the field to keep it from the WorldStopper General's grasp had been given to the mayor. It was to be the first and only exhibit in Starkley International Museum of History. Unfortunately, you couldn't really see it, as the mayor had it entirely encased in concrete.

At least, he *thought* it was concrete. Hamish suspected it *might* actually be **ZINOXYCLUMP™**...

The town looked a treat. The entire square was piled high with free sweets, thanks to Madame Cous Cous. She'd been up all night too, replacing all the cobblestones with gobstoppers.

She'd even met a new man.

'Who's this?' Clover asked her.

'This is Håkon,' she said, nestling into the enormously tall blond man, with love in her eyes. 'He's from Norway.'

When he heard that, Hamish *almost* managed a smile.

'Right,' he said, turning around. 'I think I'll go home.'

'Hamish!' someone called out behind him. 'Do you want to hang out later?'

It was his brother. He was half-smiling, looking hopeful.

'Sure,' said Hamish, giving him a little thumbs up. 'See you at home, James.'

'Actually...' said James, giving a little thumbs up back. 'Could you call me Jimmy again?'

Hamish smiled to himself. Maybe things weren't perfect, but at least life was pretty much back to normal in Starkley.

Mum even wanted to play Boggle later. She said she'd be back early from work today, because complaints in Starkley had dropped from 3,414 a week to just two. And both of those were from Mum herself, complaining that now she didn't have enough work to do.

Maybe Hamish would walk past Slackjaw's Motors on the way home. Mr Slackjaw had seemed very pleased with Hamish lately. He'd even offered him a Saturday job when he was older. Since the rebellion, sales of Vespas were up five hundred per cent! Dad had always said a Saturday job was an important thing. And maybe he could plant a few more of his sunflower seeds on his way home.

Just for the future. Just in case.

And then the strangest thing happened.

From nowhere, and almost silently, a blackbird landed on the pavement right in front of Hamish.

It looked up at him.

Now I don't know what it looks like when a bird smiles, but surely birds must smile sometimes . . . and maybe this was one of those times.

It blinked its eyes and tilted its head to one side.

'That's weird,' said Alice.

Hamish frowned and leaned forward for a closer look.

'The Blackbird,' said a tall and willowy woman, who Hamish was certain hadn't been there before. He didn't recognise her at all. 'That's what we used to call him.'

Hamish and Alice looked at the stranger. She was dressed in white. She had straight blonde hair, tucked neatly back behind one ear. Sharp blue eyes. A long, straight nose.

'I'm sorry?' said Hamish.

'In the Before – we called him the Blackbird.'

The kids looked at each other. This nutter was making very little sense.

'Okay . . .' said Alice, gently. 'Who? Who did you call the Blackbird?'

The woman smiled.

'Your father, Hamish,' she said.

Hamish went white.

'My dad?' he said, quietly and cautiously. 'You knew my dad?'

'I *know* your dad,' she said. 'I've known him since the Before.'

'Who are you?' said Alice.

'I'm a friend,' said the woman. 'I'm no one.'

'What do you mean, in the Before?' said Hamish, as she guided them to a bench and sat with them. 'Before what?'

'Before the Events,' she said. 'Your father helped start the Uprising. The WorldStoppers wanted him finished. That's why they came to Starkley. For him.'

'My dad . . . is in sales,' said Hamish, still not quite knowing what that meant.

'I'm also in . . . sales,' she said, and he noticed the small black logo on her top. A sunflower, flanked by wings. 'I work with your dad at Belasko. The stories he told you – the ones that secretly you thought he made up? They were all true, Hamish.'

She caught herself.

'Except for that one about being followed by a bunch of

320

angry Romanian spies around a Holiday Inn. That was utter nonsense, though it was *based* on a true story, I suppose.'

Hamish was having trouble computing all of this.

'Where is he?' said Hamish. 'If you know my dad, where is he?'

'They used to keep him where they kept the others. The ones you rescued. He was in the last cell along. He'd scratched a blackbird into the wall in case you ever followed his clues.'

'His clues?'

'He gave you a Shepherd,' she said, looking at Alice. 'He made sure there were others like you.'

She pointed at Buster and Venk and Elliot and Clover, all polishing their medals and grinning.

'He gave you a watch. And he tried to warn you when things were grave.'

'The birds,' said Hamish, remembering the blackbird in the garden, the one in town, the one at the window . . .

'He loves you, Hamish. But your dad had to go.'

'Where?' said Hamish, desperately.

'He had to help the Neverpeople.'

And then a loud and furious voice came from absolutely nowhere, echoing around town and leaving fear in its wake.

'GRENVILLE BILE, WHAT ARE YOU DOING OUT HERE, BOY?'

Everyone flinched. It was the Postmaster! That fearsome brute Tubitha Bile! She stormed into the square, dragging her enormous burnt-out post office trolley behind her. Her face was bright red and she pointed one fat sausage finger at her son, accusingly.

'I'm sorry, Mum!' whimpered Grenville. 'But remember – I was getting a medal because of the quite important international incident that had far-reaching global ramifications, and—'

'Yes, yes, I know!' she said, ruffling his hair. 'I'm just worried you'll get a cold, you silly biscuit!'

She laughed, kindly. Everyone was stunned. No one had heard her laugh kindly in *ages*.

'I brought you a jumper, Grenville. And a hotdog! And a hamburger. Oh, and some nachos, because I know how much you love Mexican food . . . *El Gamba*!'

She winked at her boy, then turned to the crowd.

Everyone was just staring at her.

'Well, don't you all look lovely! And that reminds me! I'm only late because I found a whole bunch of parcels and presents meant for every single one of you! *Thousands* of them! A whole roomful! Honestly, what am I like? I'd forget my own head if it wasn't screwed on!'

Alice laughed.

'Well, there you go!' she said, shaking her head.

But Hamish had more on his mind.

'Who are the Neverpeople?' he said, turning back to the mysterious woman.

But she was nowhere to be seen.

Gone.

Vanished.

'Who did she say she was?' Hamish asked.

'She said she was no one,' Alice replied.

'That's a weird thing to say,' he said. *'No one.'*

Hamish and Alice put their hands on their hips and just stared at each other. They had no idea what to do next.

And, as they shrugged and began to walk towards the party and the sweets and the presents and the medals, Hamish heard a strange and joyful tune from somewhere just behind him.

It was birdsong.

And there, on the bench, sat the blackbird again.

And in its mouth was a small piece of white card, folded once.

Hamish kneeled down and gently took the card from the bird's beak.

'What is it?' asked Alice, as the blackbird launched itself

into the bright blue sky. 'What does it say?'

Hamish read it and frowned.

'It's an address,' he said.

**NO. 1 ARCADIAN LANE
LONDON**

Alice took it from him.

'No. 1,' she said. 'Doesn't that look like . . . *No One*?'

Hamish smiled.

He had an address.

Maybe far from being the end, this was the *start* of something.

The brass band struck up again.

And, from somewhere far above, a blackbird called.

PROUD ORGAN OF BRITAIN'S LEAST MOST BORING TOWN

Starkley Post

December 22st Thursday 2015 vol 7 issue Xii

PRICE 7°

TOWN CLOCK RUNS ON TIME!

In a shocking turn of events, the town clock suddenly started keeping the correct time this week.

"At precisely 12 o'clock," said a witness, "the clock said it was precisely 12 o'clock!"

"I have never seen the like," added a man who'd never seen the like.

RECORD MONTH FOR EXCLAMATION MARKS!

More exclamation marks have been used in editions of the Starkley Post than ever before, says editor Rhona Framp.

"It's amazing! Everything's changed! In the old days sometimes we couldn't even bear to finish sentences because they were so boring! But nowadays, everything ends like this!"

And it's true! Look!! That sentence had two exclamation marks!!! And that one had *three!!!!*

And now we're using ITALICS! And we're *CAPITALISING* THEM!!!!!!!!!

STARKLEY "MOST EXCITING BORING TOWN TO LIVE!"

Starkley's won yet another gong, after it beat stiff competition from Urkley, Thunk and Sniffleton to take the coveted "Most Exciting Boring Town To Live" award.

"While it's very exciting to win," said a spokesperson, "it's also very predictable that we did. Which I think sums Starkley up in a nutshell."

The judges said Starkley won "mainly because it was recently over run by monsters who broke all known rules of space and time."

Urkley came second for its new potato recycling scheme.

OFFICIAL: EVERYTHING'S NOT RUBBISH!

Contrary to recent reports, everything is NOT rubbish, said everyone today.

"Everything's NOT rubbish!" they said, all at once.

"I agree," said someone else. "I don't know what we were thinking!" Reports that everything was rubbish have now been rubbished.

Complaints Department
Critical Path Schedule Report

Starkley Complaints Department of the Year

90
90
00
00
00
900
800
700
,600
,500
,400
,300
,200
1,100
1,000
900
800
700
600
500
400
300
200
100

M   J   J   A   S   O   N   D

Where were you?

Time **day** Date **25th**
Name **Colin Robinson**
Address **12 Elderberry Ave**

Hi! We tried to deliver **All your christmas and birthday presents from last year**

We've left them **all over your garden**

We particularly liked **the swingball set from Nan**

Love **The Postmaster.**

STARKLEY MAIL

HAMISH ELLERBY
SAYS THANK YOU

Local hero Hamish Ellerby has saved the world, but says he couldn't have made it into a book without a bit of help.

First up were local literary agents Robert Kirby and Ariella Feiner, "for helping me use the word processor in the library".

Door-to-door saleswoman Laura Hough and Elisa Offord (a local marketing guru and pamphleteer) were also thanked, "for putting up posters and ringing bookshops". Lauren Ace was thanked for bothering the editors of the *Starkley Post* and the *Frinkley*

Examiner every day. EB Wallace was thanked for reading it first.

But even bigger thanks were saved for curly-haired oddball Jamie Littler "for doing brilliant doodles because I forgot to take my camera," while Hamish saved HUGE thanks for both Paul Coomey "for making all the pages and cover look so blooming exciting and cool!" and local boffin Jane Griffiths "for her great ideas and brilliant mind".

And his final thanks were to YOU - for reading it!

Go to **worldofhamish.com**
NOW to find out more
about Hamish and Danny,
join the PDF, watch
exclusive videos PLUS
the chance to enter
special competitions!